KU-225-178

PRINCESS OLIVIA INVESTIGATES:
THE WRONG WEATHER

LUCY HAWKING
ILLUSTRATED BY ZOE PERSICO

PUFFIN

PUFFIN BOOKS

UK | USA | Canada | Ireland | Australia
India | New Zealand | South Africa

Puffin Books is part of the Penguin Random House group of companies
whose addresses can be found at global.penguinrandomhouse.com.

www.penguin.co.uk   www.puffin.co.uk   www.ladybird.co.uk

First published 2022
001

Text copyright © Lucy Hawking, 2022
Illustrations copyright © Zoe Persico, 2022

The moral right of the author and illustrator has been asserted

Typeset in Baskerville
Printed and bound in Great Britain by Clays Ltd, Elcograf S.p.A.

The authorized representative in the EEA is Penguin Random House Ireland,
Morrison Chambers, 32 Nassau Street, Dublin D02 YH68

A CIP catalogue record for this book is available from the British Library

ISBN: 978–0–241–48512–5

All correspondence to:
Puffin Books
Penguin Random House Children's
One Embassy Gardens, 8 Viaduct Gardens, London SW11 7BW

Penguin Random House is committed to a
sustainable future for our business, our readers
and our planet. This book is made from Forest
Stewardship Council® certified paper.

To all the Princess Olivias in the world

PROLOGUE

From the top of the lookout tower, Princess Olivia could see for miles across the mountainous landscape of the kingdom that would one day be hers. It was just before her third birthday and she was so small that her father, King Tolemy the Thirty-Second, had to lift her up to see over the old stone wall of the rampart. Peering over the edge, firmly held by her dad, she could see the wooded darkness of the quiet mountains, broken in places by yellowy green spring leaves and rushing torrents of pale blue water from the distant glacier. Mist hung low across the quiet landscape.

'**Look**,' said her father, the king, as he pointed down below the ancient lookout tower to a huge tree. It had spreading branches covered in delicate pale pink flowers whose petals curled upwards to greet the morning sunlight. 'Do you remember the story of that tree?'

Princess Olivia smiled and shook her head, even though she did. She wanted to hear her father tell her again about the special tree, the emblem of the kingdom of Alez. She sighed happily as he began the tale.

'A thousand years ago,' he said, his breath

2

softly tickling the back of her ear, 'our ancestors came across the glacier from the other side. Back then, no one knew what lay beyond those mountains.' In the distance, Olivia could see the jagged rocky edges of the grey peaks that lay in a semi-circle round the kingdom.

'It was **a huge adventure**,' said her father. 'People came here to escape. A horde of terrifying horseback warriors had swept across the continent on the other side of the mountains, seizing control of everywhere they passed through. Only by climbing over the glacier, where they knew the invaders wouldn't follow them, did our ancestors get to safety. They followed the honey scent of this land across the ice to find the valley. Do you know who led them?'

He smiled down at his bright-eyed, clever daughter who, even at the age of nearly three, he sometimes felt had already sorted her world into better order than he had managed to as an adult.

'Yes!' said Olivia. 'But **tell me again, Papa!**'

'King Tolemy the First!' said her dad.

'The same as you!' Olivia joined in.

'Exactly! The great king I'm named after! He founded Alez. When he saw that tree –' he pointed – 'which is called . . .?'

He gave his daughter a quizzical look and she giggled, a sound he loved more than anything in the world.

'**The angel tree!**' burst out Olivia. 'The angel tree breathes on the kingdom, and that keeps it safe!'

'Clever girl! When Tolemy the First saw the angel tree, he stuck his sword into the earth beneath it and said that, from now on, Alez would be a kingdom of peace and beauty where everyone could live safely and **be happy!**'

'Everyone be happy,' echoed Olivia, twisting round to beam up at her dad. 'With our angel tree!'

'While the angel tree flowers, no harm can come to Alez or any of the subjects who live here,' said her dad. 'And it's our job, as the royal family, to keep it that way.'

CHAPTER 1
Six years later . . .

Olivia was in the royal library, curled into one of the huge leather armchairs with her blanket and her best teddy, reading an old book about the palace. She was trying to plan an **escape route**. Turning the heavy pages, she sighed – but not happily. She wanted to find a map of the palace buildings and grounds to see whether she could find a secret way out that she hadn't come across before.

She'd already tried everything she could think of. Once, she had nearly got out of a small gate in the huge walls that surrounded the palace grounds. The gate had been hidden by such a thick coat of ivy that no one but her had realized it was there. She'd managed to push it open but only walked a few paces outside when she heard footsteps behind her. Nina, her nanny, had caught her and brought her back before she could get even a glimpse of the world outside. The guards had blocked the gate the next day.

After that escape attempt, Nina had felt sorry for lonely Olivia and brought her a set of brightly covered paperback books, which Olivia kept stuffed into her duvet cover to read endlessly at night by the light of a torch. In the dim light of the little bulb, she read about the exciting adventures of two girls in a faraway land called England. They went to a **boarding school** and became **detectives**. Olivia really, *really* wished she could go to school and be a detective. Sitting up at night in her four-poster bed with the embroidered curtains and her favourite teddy bear, Prince George, she imagined what school would be like, how many friends she would have and the mysteries she would solve there.

But that was just a dream world to Olivia, who lived in a palace that felt like a prison. It was a beautiful palace. Or at least, people were always *saying* it was. *She* thought it was echoey, cold and smelled of mothballs. To her, it was the **loneliest** place on Earth, despite all the bustle that filled the corridors and the hundreds of rooms. There were no other children and the grown-ups ignored her, though she knew if she tried to escape again, they would come running after her straight away.

And there was hardly anything to do, except have her lessons with the tutors who came to teach her pointless things like the lute and table manners – subjects that her parents thought were **important** for **a young princess** but Olivia found very boring. She went on long walks around the gardens, wishing she could leave the palace grounds and find out what life was really like in the world beyond its tall walls and gates.

She hadn't been outside for years now. There had been no more trips to the lookout tower, no picnics in the mountains nor chances to paddle in the streams in the valley. When she asked her parents why they never went anywhere, her mother pretended she hadn't heard and her dad looked sad but said nothing.

That sunny morning, as the butterflies

fluttered and the hummingbirds drank nectar from the mass of flowering trees outside the library window, Olivia gave up closely examining maps of the palace and decided to go back to her self-made educational system. Her parents never told her anything she wanted to know – they just banged on about royal family history and the great magical yarns of the past. Olivia felt she was **too old** now for **fairy tales** and anyway, she'd heard all the stories of Alez of the past. She wanted to know about Alez of the *present*, but her parents didn't have anything to say on that topic. Olivia was baffled by this – they told her it was her destiny to rule over Alez and yet they didn't seem able to tell her the **simplest facts** about the country they expected her to run one distant day!

To make up for this, she had come up with a plan to read everything in the library – from one side to the other. The books weren't always helpful, though. It was the library of her royal ancestors, so it was mostly about learning to joust or how to conduct complicated royal relationships with other countries.

Some, however, *were* interesting. She especially liked the **little book of maps**, where Alez was drawn and photographed in minute detail: every orchard, village and rushing stream was brilliantly coloured and recorded. She would pore for hours over the illustrations of bright blue lakes, clear rivers, green grazing pastures and huge rolling forests. Below the palace a road led to the city's port and harbour, with the sea stretching into the distance. Behind was the jagged rocky border with their next-door country, divided from Alez by the mass of the **huge icy glacier** her ancestors had once crossed. It had all been ruled over by Olivia's family for the past thousand years.

Over Olivia's head, as she sat in her armchair, hung a scowling portrait of her great-grandmother, the terrifying grande marquessa. She was **so frightening** even the artist hadn't dared paint her with a smile. From the picture, Olivia could see she had the same snub nose as her great-grandmother but she often thought how lucky the grande marquessa was not to wear glasses like she did, as the marquessa really didn't have the right kind of nose to keep them

in place. She had the same wide-spaced, shiny eyes, the same sweep of hair that fell forward and the same heart-shaped face ending in a determined chin; in the portrait this was raised in exactly the way Olivia raised her own when she wanted to ask a question.

Olivia could even see that, like her, the grande marquessa was not a large person. The biggest difference was that where Olivia's face always wanted to break into a **smile**, her great-grandmother's mouth was turned down into a **scowl**.

What the painter couldn't capture was the grande marquessa's legendary voice, said to be so commanding that even the birds stopped singing when she spoke. Olivia liked to try out scary voices to see if she could come up with one good enough for the grande marquessa. But just as Olivia was scary-voicing her way through a long and confusing paragraph about how to politely declare war on a badly behaved nearby country, something happened.

Suddenly she heard a **commotion** coming from the Great Throne Room next door! She jumped out of her big armchair and ran to the connecting door to peek through.

From her side view, she could see her mum and dad, lolling in their thrones as usual with their crowns on. But instead of a whole host of servants around them, fussing and whispering and jostling to get closer to the royal couple, a very different group of people – ones Olivia had never seen before – had barged noisily in.

This was all **extremely odd**. Ordinary people were not supposed to speak until they were spoken to, and they certainly weren't meant to charge around the royal rooms, examining priceless objects, toppling huge flower arrangements and helping themselves to sandwiches.

The crowd was dressed in unfamiliar clothes. Usually, everyone in Alez – by law – wore the national dress, which for non-royal people was a knee-length embroidered wraparound garment with socks and sandals. But this group were wearing strange, two-piece costumes made of black cloth with leg coverings that went right down to their shoes and a square jacket that buttoned at the front. Both men and women were dressed the same; under the black jackets, they wore white shirts with an odd-looking narrow red piece of fabric tied round their necks, which hung in a straight line down their fronts.

Olivia could see her parents were **not coping well** without her. She pushed her way through the black-clad crowd, not even bothering to say 'please' or 'excuse me'. For a second, she thought she needed Prince George, her loyal and supportive teddy bear, but there was no

time to go and get him, so she ducked and dived over to the two thrones and was just about to give her dad a hug when a man and a woman walked forward, and the crowd went quiet.

'Paragona and Tolemy,' the large, heavyset man said, not even bothering to bow. Those were the names of Olivia's parents, but no one ever said them because they were supposed to address them only as 'Your Royal Majesties'.

Olivia's dad, King Tolemy the Thirty-Second, looked around wildly for his courtiers to tell him what on earth was going on. But **everyone had vanished**.

'Minister Jeremy Pont!' said Tolemy in confusion. 'What in the name of the angel tree of Alez do you mean by this! Deputy Minister Gretchen Sparks! You too? I thought we worked together and trusted each other!'

Jeremy smiled. 'We're here to help,' he said, tipping his head in what almost looked like a bow but wasn't. The group behind him, silent now and standing in a long row, nodded solemnly.

'Help?' said Tolemy, sounding even more perplexed. Paragona's mouth was wide open in an expression of horror. Olivia knew this meant things were really bad, as usually her mother forbade such facial expressions as 'common' or 'ageing'.

'Yes,' said Gretchen, the deputy minister soothingly. 'We realize that you have borne the **terrible burden** of the crown for so long.'

The group behind them put sorrowful expressions on their faces.

'And it's too much for you now. We, the people of Alez, can no longer expect that you suffer the pain and stress of running this country – especially not with its present challenges, which you are so ill-equipped to meet,' she continued as Jeremy turned away briefly to answer his mobile phone. Olivia clocked this. She knew about mobile phones because she'd once found her nanny, Nina, using one in secret to call home, but Nina had refused to let her play with it as mobile phones were banned inside the palace.

'It's **not your fault**,' Jeremy added in a syrupy voice, tucking his phone into his pocket. 'You tried. You went along with the decisions we told you to take. But nothing has prepared you for the complex nature of the modern world.'

Olivia was looking from Jeremy to her parents and trying to work out what was happening. Disloyal though it felt, she knew this intruder was right. After all, her parents didn't even have their own mobile phones so they couldn't call for back-up now they needed it! What else was missing from the life of the palace? How far behind were they really?

'What . . . what's going to happen now?' said her father meekly.

'We're going to take over from you, let you have a really nice, good rest,' said Jeremy firmly. 'We're going to get everything sorted out, those tiresome problems that you found so difficult to manage. The big mistakes you've made. Once we have the whole situation under control, we can give you a call or maybe pop in to let you know how everything's going?'

'Pop in?' said the king. 'What do you mean?'

'Didn't I say?' said Jeremy, in what Olivia just knew was fake surprise. 'We're going to need the palace as the new seat of government. It's just perfect, so it's time for you to **go somewhere else**.'

'But where?' said the king in bewilderment. 'Wh-wh-wh–?' he stuttered. But he didn't get an answer as he was already being helped out of his throne by members of the crowd.

Queen Paragona still looked too stunned to speak as Gretchen took her gently by the hand and led her towards the great doors.

Only Olivia seemed able to say anything.

'You're throwing us out of our house?' she piped up. She tried for the grande marquessa scary voice, but it came out much more squeakily. '**You can't do that!**'

Jeremy Pont turned his gaze on her. He had eyes the colour of the cloudy azure blue of the icy streams that ran down from the Alez glacier, way up in the mountains behind the palace.

Olivia shivered; she suddenly felt afraid.

'Little girl,' said Jeremy. 'Your people have lived off the fat of this land for over a thousand years – and look what a mess it's become. Don't you think it's time to let someone who knows what they are doing rule the country?'

'A mess?' said Olivia, perplexed. 'Why is it a mess? I don't understand.'

'You will,' said Jeremy. 'Guards, escort them out of the palace grounds. Take them to the bus stop. From there, they can arrange their own transport to the city to start their **new lives**.'

As Olivia and her parents stumbled out of the palace, no one would meet their gaze. Even the gardeners, once so friendly, turned away as they passed. But just as they got to the big gates, they heard running footsteps behind them. Out of breath, Nina, Olivia's nanny – well, ex-nanny now, it seemed – ran up to them and pressed a pillowcase full of clanking objects into Paragona's hands.

'It was all I could grab,' she said, panting and looking back to see if anyone was watching her. 'I must go! Prince George is in the bag! And your book of Alez!' She kissed Olivia on the forehead and disappeared into the trees by the gate.

Now clutching the oddly shaped pillowcase – which turned out to have a selection of Paragona's jewels and crowns in it as well as Olivia's precious bear and her treasured book of pictures – the royal family stood silently at the bus stop at the end of the long palace drive while several buses roared past.

They didn't know they had to put a hand out to make one stop.

Eventually **a saggy old bus** wheezed to a halt in front of them, and so the three ex-royals clambered on and took their seats in the front row. The bus cranked into life and set off down the winding roads towards the great port city of Alez. Olivia had never been there before and certainly never expected to visit the city in an ancient bus, puffing out great clouds of black smoke behind it, while she sat squeezed between her parents on ripped seats looking out of dirty windows.

Olivia's parents were startled beyond belief by this unexpected turn of events. Paragona was even too taken aback to examine her **jewellery collection**, something that at other times would have been her first priority. Tolemy was clearly lost in a nightmare. But Olivia was peering out for her first proper glimpse of the world beyond the palace gates. Finally she was escaping! But not in the way she had ever expected. And what she saw was a surprise too.

The books of old photos and pictures in the library had shown the road down to Alez City as lined with happy villages, flowering angel trees and smiling children. But instead, Olivia could now see that the roads were littered with little shacks made of plastic, branches and corrugated iron. The trees had thin drooping branches with only yellow leaves that drifted downwards to the scrubby earth. Skinny children stood around in groups, poking at

mangy-looking cats. Dirty water pooled in puddles that glowed with an eerie shimmer. As the bus turned a bend and the city below laid itself out like a living map, Olivia could see the harbour definitely did not hold tall ships with fluttering sails and brilliant flags – as she'd seen in her book – but the rusted hulks of abandoned vessels.

The weather, which had been bright and sunny as they had stood at the bus stop, suddenly closed in and the old bus was buffeted by high winds and squalls of fierce rain so dense that Olivia could see nothing but **fat raindrops** running down the windows. Was this the start of the adventure she had longed for? Torn between excitement and surprise, she hugged her bear closer and wondered what the outside world was going to reveal to her, now she was about to be part of it.

CHAPTER 2
One month later . . .

'**I'm not wearing a crown to school!**'
Olivia said hotly, trying to wriggle away as her
mother plaited her hair. 'Not my first day, my
second day or any day. Ever. **E.V.E.R!**'

She spelled it out in case her mother hadn't
got the message.

'Olivia,' her mother pleaded as she tried to roll and pin Olivia's long curly braids. Olivia had always hated wearing her crown, so her mother had been coming up with inventive hairstyles to keep it fixed on since Olivia was a very small girl.

'**No**,' said Olivia, standing up abruptly and pulling the pins out of her hair. 'No one else will be wearing a crown at school, so why should I?'

'**Of course they won't!**' cried her mother. 'Because no one else is a **princess!**'

'And neither,' said Olivia sternly, 'am I.'

Her mother gave a little gasp and fluttered her hands in the air. 'We may be in changed circumstances,' she said, 'but we can still do our duty as royal people! And your duty is to be the future of Alez!'

Olivia's heart sank. She couldn't see any way in their 'changed circumstances' that she could possibly be the future of Alez. Wherever the future was, it probably wasn't arguing about princess crowns with its mother.

From the doorway of Olivia's room, her father said mildly, 'Olivia, you will always be a princess, no matter what anyone says.'

'What about **a tiny tiara?**' said her mother, rifling through the pillowcase where she still kept all her jewels. 'Like this!' She held up a narrow gold circlet with just a few sparkly gems in it. 'It's so discreet!' she said. 'Absolutely right for a young princess on her first day at –' she swallowed – 'school!'

She looked at Olivia hopefully. And Olivia thought she could see tears in the corners of her mother's eyes, glinting like the little stones in her crown.

'OK,' said Olivia reluctantly, but only because she didn't want her mother to cry.

Her mother's face brightened instantly.

'But I'm wearing my dungarees,' she warned.

'I'm not putting that dress on.' She eyed a long frilly pink dress that her mother had draped over the chair in her room.

Over the last few weeks, since they had got on that bus and rumbled away from their life at the palace, Olivia had been carefully **monitoring the weather** out of the windows of their tiny apartment, writing down notes in a little notebook. Her favourite uncle, Cassander, had given it to her for her 'new life' at school. Taking notes had turned out to be a full-time job for Olivia as the weather seemed to **change constantly**. It was sunny and boiling hot one moment, but then suddenly it would cloud over

and a huge storm would break, raining bright streaks of lightning down on to the abandoned ships in the bay.

That particular morning, Olivia had noticed a pattern of **dark clouds** coming towards the coast from the mountains. While she knew she couldn't predict the weather, she certainly didn't want to be out in a long frilly dress in a hailstorm – or in a freak heatwave. Or both at the same time.

Her mother's shoulders sagged.

'Let her, Paragona,' counselled her father from the doorway. 'She's been through more than enough already.'

'It's ridiculous that she has to go to this school!' protested the former queen. 'I just can't bear it!'

Olivia gave herself a small smile in the mirror. Her parents had been **horrified** when the letter from the authorities had arrived, addressed to 'Mr and Mrs Alez', informing them their nine-year-old daughter was required **by law** to attend the **local primary school**, just like every other child in the new Republic of Alez. Her parents were appalled – and Olivia was absolutely **thrilled!**

Despite her high hopes and comfy dungarees, Olivia's first day didn't get off to a good start.

Olivia and her mother didn't realize how long it would take them to walk from their new apartment to the school, and so they were late. Paragona was so used to being driven everywhere in a shiny car with motorcycles flashing their blue lights and speeding alongside them that she thought every journey took around ten minutes. In fact, it took half an hour to cover the distance from their new home to school on foot.

Paragona's high-heeled shoes didn't help. There were a surprising number of **potholes** and **broken paving slabs**, so Olivia – who was wearing plimsolls – had to keep picking up her mum when she tripped over.

The other thing that was still surprising to Olivia was that everywhere was so *dirty*. Up at the mountaintop palace, the air was thin and clear. Sunshine sparkled on the streams of water. The trees and shrubs sprouted glossy, healthy leaves with brilliant-coloured flowers sending their scent into the air to attract plump bumblebees and butterflies.

But here in the city below, everything looked very different. The cloud cover was getting thicker every day and was now so dense that Olivia couldn't see the sky for the heavy mass of **grey-brown smog** over her head. When she'd looked out from her bedroom window at the palace, she often saw these clouds, hiding the valley and the sea beyond from view. From up on high, she liked to imagine that the palace floated on a bed of puffy clouds, like a magical kingdom in the sky. She realized she had never thought about what it might be like to be underneath those clouds, unable to see the Sun.

She plodded along the streets, trying to prop up her mother who was getting dirtier and more dishevelled the longer they walked through the dense city streets. It was hailing now, thin painful shards of ice slashing at their faces even though it was an uncomfortably muggy day. Olivia thought back to the books she had read about Alez in the palace library and the pictures she had seen. She couldn't know how hot or cold it was in those old photos and drawings, but at least it had looked as though it was either hot *or* cold – not both at the same time. Her mind was whirring constantly, trying to take in this mass of **new information and experiences** and match it up against her expectations. She just couldn't make sense of any of it.

It didn't help that posters of the grinning face of the new president, Jeremy Pont, seemed to follow Olivia along the grubby streets as she walked to school. Massive slogans screamed things like:

> *Jeremy Pont –*
> *a Man for All People, Not Just Some People!*

They passed a square where a huge crane was carefully setting a bronze statue of Jeremy in the place where there used to be a marble statue of Olivia's dad.

It was very clear to Olivia that the future looked more like Jeremy Pont than it looked like her.

She kept trying to shield her mother from seeing the posters and the statue for fear it would upset her further, but fortunately Paragona was so distracted by the state of her own footwear that she didn't notice anything around her.

When they finally arrived – late and very scruffy – they were shown into a building that looked **nothing** like the school in Olivia's **dreams**. From her book reading, she thought 'school' meant a sweeping front drive, flowering creepers, stained-glass windows and possibly a few ponies in the background.

Instead, it turned out to be a series of interconnecting low flat-roofed buildings set on dusty land, surrounded by a chain-link security fence. There was a playground on one side but there wasn't much to play on, just a few broken swings and some trees whose skeleton leaves were only just clinging on to the branches. To one side of the playground, on the other side of the chain fence, a group of old women sat with baskets and large boxes. They seemed to be waiting. Olivia had no idea for what.

Once inside, matters got a whole lot worse. A laid-back-looking man with a shaved head arrived to collect Olivia at reception and said how pleased he was to have her join his class. Olivia's mother bristled immediately. This young man was not her idea of the perfect tutor. He was wearing shorts and a T-shirt! Round his neck was a lanyard with his name on it. Olivia hadn't seen a name that looked so long and tricky to pronounce before. He smiled at Olivia as if he could read her mind and just said, '**Call me Mr V**. Everyone else does.'

Olivia was as surprised as her mother was that this was what teachers looked like, but tried to hide it as she followed Mr V to the classroom.

Paragona insisted on joining them.

Mr V raised his eyebrows and said it really wasn't necessary, at which point Paragona drew herself up to her full height – which was impressive as she was rather tall, much more so than Mr V anyway – and haughtily said it was absolutely necessary. Unfortunately, her fierceness was ruined by the fact that she had some **rubbish stuck to her crown** and her flouncy, ruffled golden dress was covered in dirt down one side. Paragona had resisted all Olivia's attempts to get her to dress 'normally' and insisted on parading one of her state occasion dresses instead.

Olivia winced and Mr V gave her a sympathetic look.

'Of course,' he said. 'Come this way.'

He showed them into the classroom where

rows of upturned faces gazed back at Olivia, none of them smiling. Behind the students hung a huge banner with a photo of Jeremy Pont on it. He was everywhere! Next to his stern face was written in huge loopy writing:

Giving Alez the future it deserves! Your President JP, A man for All People, not just some people!

Mr V was about to introduce Olivia when Paragona stepped forward, her majesty semi-intact despite the festooning of mud and debris and announced, '**Class! Please stand!**'

Olivia's heart plunged to the tips of her toes.

Grumbling and shuffling, the students got to their feet, noisily pushing each other, pinching and whispering to one another.

'And now, **greet Princess Olivia** in the proper fashion,' said Paragona imperiously. 'As her loyal subjects of the Kingdom of Alez!' She threw her arms up in a show of enthusiasm, which caused her crown to fall over one eye.

Olivia wanted the ground to open up and swallow her.

No one obeyed her mother.

'Greet the Princess, I command you!' insisted Paragona, stamping her foot, which sent her flying off balance as it broke the heel of her shoe.

The children giggled while Olivia turned a brilliant shade of red. But one child, sitting near the end of the front row of desks, who had **butterfly wings** pinned to the back of his school jumper, came out from behind his desk to the front and faced Olivia.

'Ravi!' shouted all the other children. 'Don't do it! She's not a princess!'

But Ravi just smiled. For a second, it looked as

though he might bow to Princess Olivia, but then he held out his clenched hand instead.

Olivia felt even more confused. Paragona looked on in astonishment.

Ravi took her hand, gently closed the fingers and then bumped his own fist against hers.

'Princess, ' he said softly, looking straight into Olivia's grey eyes, **now brimming with tears** behind her glasses. 'Come and sit with me.'

He ushered Olivia to the spare desk next to him and tucked her into her new seat on the end of the row while Mr V was still helping Olivia's mother up off the floor.

'Thank you,' Olivia said in the tiniest of voices.

Ravi smiled and winked. 'You'll be OK – just stick with me.'

A very **serious-looking girl** with a heavy fringe stood up from the row behind and addressed Paragona directly. The former queen was now back on her feet – but a bit lopsidedly, as she only had one high-heeled shoe on.

'My mum says that monarchy is a tool of oppression handed down through the centuries to reinforce the power of the ruling classes to profiteer from the sweat of others. And –'

'**Thank you, Helga**,' said Mr V hastily. But Helga could not be stopped.

'And Mama says that now is the time when we can start to redress the wrongs of the past and retell our history from the side of those who have been downtrodden.'

'Goodness,' said Paragona rather faintly. 'How very . . . interesting . . .'

She looked around her in a panic and saw that Olivia had sat down next to the strikingly handsome boy who had curtseyed so beautifully. Paragona was about to protest further, but the look on her daughter's face stopped even her.

Go. Now! Olivia mouthed at her mother.

'Why don't you get back to reception where you can have a little sit-down and a rest?' Mr V said soothingly.

'A rest, yes,' said her mother gratefully,

hobbling towards the door and vanishing through it very fast with just a small sob escaping her lips. Olivia sank further into her seat.

Mr V turned to face his class.

'Now, good morning, students!' he said. 'I've got an announcement to make!'

The class rustled and shuffled excitedly.

'We,' said Mr V with a flourish, 'have been told to start making preparations for –' he brought up a large image on the whiteboard of a water pump – '**Day Zero!** Who can tell me? What is Day Zero?'

Olivia's neighbour shot his hand up in the air.

'Ravi,' said Mr V, looking pleased. 'Would you like to share?'

Ravi stood up and faced the other students.

'Day Zero,' he said in his confident, musical voice, 'will be the day our water supply runs out! The day we start standing in line at the water pumps to get our daily ration.'

He sat down again. Olivia felt her scalp prickle in horror. The *water* supply was running out? What about the **big glacier** in the mountains, the one her ancestors had climbed over and had ever since had protected Alez from intruders and provided it with clean flowing water?

'Absolutely!' beamed Mr V, as though he was announcing the class was invited to a party, not just telling them that the country was running out of water. 'Day Zero means our taps will no longer run with water. Already, we know that we have to be careful with water. What do we already do to save water?'

A girl in the back row put her hand in the air. 'Adanna,' said Mr V.

'We don't waste water,' she said. 'We don't flush the toilet every time. We reuse water when we can. It's **illegal** to have **a bath**.'

Olivia gasped. Her mother spent hours in hot baths, filling up several times before she got out.

'And –' Adanna went to carry on, but suddenly she started wheezing. She bent double while Mr V rushed over to her and grabbed an object from her bag, which she attached to her mouth and inhaled rapidly. Mr V carefully got her into her seat and waited until her breath went back to normal. And then he returned to the front of the class and carried on, as though nothing unusual had happened. Olivia couldn't believe that everyone just ignored the girl who had suddenly seemed to run out of breath. She wanted to ask Ravi, but Mr V was in full flow once more.

'One other thing I need you to know,' said their teacher. 'We've been asked by the government to inform everyone that **the tap water is no longer drinkable**. From now on, I want you to remember a really simple phrase – and tell it to your parents too!'

Mr V flicked up a new slide, which showed a

family happily drinking water from plastic bottles. The words 'Bottled or Boiled!' were written in huge loopy letters next to the joyful faces of the family, enjoying their sips of water.

'Let's say it together!' said Mr V enthusiastically. 'Come on, everyone – on three! One, two, three!'

'Bottled or Boiled,' mumbled the class, except for Ravi, whose voice rose clear above the rest.

'**Louder!**' cried Mr V, who seemed to Olivia to want to make every single moment of anything that happened fun, regardless of whether it actually was or not.

'**Bottled or boiled!**' shouted the class.

'Remember, we only drink water that has been bottled or boiled!' said Mr V. 'Think of it as the new school motto!'

Olivia's family had a motto, which had been written in gold letters over every door in the palace, but it definitely wasn't 'Bottled or Boiled'. It was 'Courageous Be the Prince Who Taketh the Green Mountain' or something. It had been translated from the ancient Alez language of her ancestors. Olivia didn't think this would be a good moment to mention it.

'Great,' said Mr V, smiling. 'Later, we'll have a **water-pump drill** so we can practise standing in line for our **water rations**! And now on to our next topic . . .'

A question popped into Olivia's mind, and she put her small hand up in the air. She had to wave it around a few times to catch Mr V's attention, but finally he spotted her.

'Olivia,' he said, smiling. 'What is it?'

'Um,' said Olivia squeakily, wishing her voice would come out as strong and clear as Ravi's. 'You didn't say. Why?'

Mr V's face fell as the class whistled.

'I don't know what you mean,' he said, wrinkling his brow.

Olivia realized the other students were staring at her now. She felt a bit shocked that she was causing a commotion just by asking a question. But she had to carry on.

'**Why?**' she said. 'Why can't we drink the tap water? Why is the water running out?'

'Olivia,' said Mr V kindly. 'It's good to ask questions – but only *some* questions. Why don't you come and find me at the staff room one break time, and we'll have a chat. Very good! Let's move on, class. It's time to sing the national anthem . . .'

Olivia's head sank forward on to her desk. She'd summoned her courage to ask the question and yet she hadn't received any kind of answer! She felt confused and upset.

Ravi nudged Olivia with his butterfly wings.

WATER SHORTAGES

by Lucy Hawking

Water is essential to life – every life form we know about needs water to survive. It's so important that scientists think that without water we would not have life on Earth. And when they look for life on other planets, they have a simple phrase: 'Follow the water.' If they find water in space, they think they might also find life!

On Earth, water seems to be everywhere – it falls from the sky, runs along in rivers, lives in lakes and oceans, and flows out of our taps.

If you've ever been caught in a rainstorm, you might find it hard to believe that the Earth has a problem with water. In fact, 70 per cent of the Earth's surface is covered with water - our beautiful blue planet has more oceans than it has land.

But we are facing a problem with water - and it's getting worse. Only a tiny amount of the water on Earth is freshwater. And we already have so many uses for that water - we drink it, wash with it, water crops with it and use it to make things.

With more and more people in the world, there is an ever-greater demand for freshwater, often in places where cities have grown enormously in recent years. Added to this, climate change is causing weather patterns to change, so more water is falling in some places, meaning huge floods happen more often. But other places are suffering terrible droughts or wildfires as the rain supply dries up – and farmers can't then grow crops or farm animals.

Much of our freshwater is now also polluted, meaning it could be dangerous to drink it or feed it to animals. Millions of people live in areas without easy access to clean, safe water and this causes many problems, especially for kids, who are more likely to get sick or miss out on school because they have to help their families to carry water, sometimes from distant wells or taps.

For these reasons, we all must try to be careful about the way we use water. This can be as simple as turning the tap off while you brush your teeth!

CAN YOU THINK OF ANOTHER WAY THAT YOU COULD SAVE WATER IN YOUR DAILY LIFE?

'Don't be sad,' he said. He put his hands on her shoulders and pulled her upright. 'And don't mind the others; they're not bad really, once you get to know them. You'll make friends.'

Olivia looked around but the other children still didn't seem very pleased to see her.

'I can be your first friend until you get some more,' added Ravi.

'Really?' said Olivia.

'You seem super nice,' said Ravi. 'And I've always wanted to be a princess, so perhaps you can teach me how.'

'I've always wanted to be a normal person,' confessed Olivia. 'And not be a princess ever again.'

'Perfect!' said Ravi. 'Then we are **best friends** already!'

Olivia sat in a daze in the classroom through the first morning session. She had **no idea** what was going on, but Ravi kept nudging her, whispering instructions and giving her quiet bits of advice. She didn't know she had to stand up and face to the east with the rest of the class while they sang the new national anthem of Alez. Not knowing the words or the tune, she just mumbled along, hoping no one would notice. The chorus to the endless verses seemed to be 'Jeremy Pont is the Greatest!' so by the end at least she could join in with that bit, even though she obviously didn't enjoy singing a song about the man who had thrown her family out of their home.

When she had lived in the palace and been so desperate to escape, she had never thought she could possibly miss the dusty, highly decorated rooms with their ornate uncomfortable sofas and their huge doors with the gold mouldings, which were almost too heavy for her to push open by herself. Suddenly, in this new, darker, more confusing world, she longed for the peace of the palace library and her ancient books, with the flowering trees outside the window. Would she ever be able to go back home? Despite wanting to know what the rest of the world was like, Olivia did still think of the palace as home. Would she have to live here forever, in the sea-level city, among the chaos, the dirt and the terrible weather?

At that moment a bell rang. At the palace, a bell at this time of day meant the big doors would fly open and a flock of servants would appear, carrying **iced jugs of lemonade** and **big plates of delicious cakes and sandwiches**. At school, it was the opposite. Everyone got up and ran out instead.

'Where are they going?' she asked Ravi. 'Is it time for the water-pump drill?'

'Break time!' sang Ravi. 'C'mon, you're

blocking the row.'

He pushed Olivia forward out of her seat, grabbed her hand and took her through the corridors into the dirty playground where most of the kids had made a beeline for the old ladies on the other side of the chain-link fence.

'What are they doing?' Olivia asked in amazement. The children were passing coins through the fence to the old ladies, who were handing them back **small greasy parcels** or **brightly coloured bottles of liquid**.

'Buying snacks,' said Ravi. 'Did you want something?'

'You shouldn't eat those things,' said Helga, who had trailed after them. 'My mums say that sort of food is bad for you.'

'*I* don't eat them!' said Ravi seriously. 'I'm a vegan. We grow all our vegetables on the balcony at home. I was just asking if the princess wanted anything.'

'She's not a princess,' said Helga disapprovingly. 'You shouldn't call her that.'

'It's OK,' said Olivia. '**You can call me Olly**. I like it better anyway.'

Olly was the nickname Uncle Cassander had given her, and Olivia had always used it as her name for herself. Even so, she still felt a small tremor of sadness pass through her that no one would ever call her 'Princess Olivia' again. She'd longed not to be a princess – and now she wasn't. She thought she ought to feel happy about it, but somehow she didn't.

'It's her first day!' said Ravi, standing on his tiptoes in a perfectly balanced move. 'Talk about something else, Helga!'

'Oh, OK. Um . . . I've got two mums.' Helga addressed Olivia directly.

'You're so lucky,' said Ravi enviously. 'I wish I did. I've only got one.'

Olivia's eyes bulged at the thought of two

Paragonas in her life. She couldn't imagine what that would be like.

They had wandered closer to where the old ladies were selling snacks.

'What *are* they eating?' said Olivia, who felt rather queasy looking at the packages the other children were scoffing.

'Meat sticks. Burgers. That kind of thing,' said Ravi airily.

Olivia thought she might cry. The snacks looked disgusting and smelled worse.

'It'll get better,' Helga said kindly. 'My first day was awful too. But I love it here now and you're going to learn about **so many cool things**.'

'I hope so,' said Olivia, touched that Helga was trying to be friendly. 'I think there's a lot I don't know.'

'Of course,' said Helga knowledgeably. 'You've been living under the yoke of imperial patriarchy, so it stands to – ouch, Ravi!!'

'Tomorrow, Helga,' said Ravi, giving her a stern look. He handed Olivia a bottle of water. 'The patriarchy can wait until tomorrow.'

'Right you are,' said Helga, nodding sagely. 'Right you are, Ravi.'

At that moment, the bell rang again for the end of break and the children started to move back towards the school building, Ravi and Helga with them. Olivia trailed after them, mouthing the word 'Pat-ree-ark-ee' and wondering what that – and everything else – would turn out to mean.

CHAPTER 3

'Question!' said Dr Mizuki, the science teacher at the front of the class that afternoon, pointing at the picture on the whiteboard. 'What comes out of the top of a volcano?!'

Helga's hand shot straight up in the air

immediately. **'Me, me, me! I know!'** She was almost hissing with excitement.

Dr Mizuki smiled at her. 'I'm going to give the others a go first. And if no one else knows, then I'll ask you, so you can put your hand down. OK?'

'OK,' said Helga reluctantly, putting her hand down slowly.

Olivia was petrified she might be picked – she had no idea what the answer was. She didn't even understand the question.

'What's a volcano?' she asked Ravi.

'Shhh,' said Ravi absent-mindedly. He was sketching in a notebook.

Helga leaned across to whisper in Olivia's ear, 'Olly, it's a natural escape route for hot material through the Earth's surface.'

'Oh,' said Olivia, confused. 'Is that a good thing?'

'Yes, in a way,' said Helga thoughtfully. 'Because they helped form **the air we breathe** and may have brought **life** to the planet.'

VOLCANOES
by Dr Isabel Fendley

A volcano is an opening in the Earth's crust.
Hot, liquid rock known as magma reaches the
surface of the Earth and erupts, sometimes
explosively. Volcanoes often form at the edges
of continental plates, which are continent-sized
pieces of rock that fit together like puzzle
pieces to make the Earth's surface. Volcanoes

at plate boundaries often form mountains, such as Mount Saint Helens in the USA, and Mount Fuji in Japan. Volcanoes can also form away from the edges of continental plates, in spots where the inside of the Earth is extra hot. These regions are known as hot spots. Volcanoes that form at hot spots often make island chains, for example the Hawaiian Islands.

Volcanic magma contains many gas bubbles, including carbon dioxide and water vapour. These bubbles push the magma up from the Earth's interior, and volcanoes form where the magma breaks through to the Earth's surface. The gases in the magma are released into the atmosphere when the volcanoes erupt.

Many billions of years ago, volcanoes were the original source of the natural carbon dioxide and many other gases in the Earth's atmosphere. However, in the present day, volcanoes release much less carbon dioxide into the atmosphere. It's actually human activities that release far more carbon dioxide into the atmosphere. Too much, in fact – to detrimental levels.

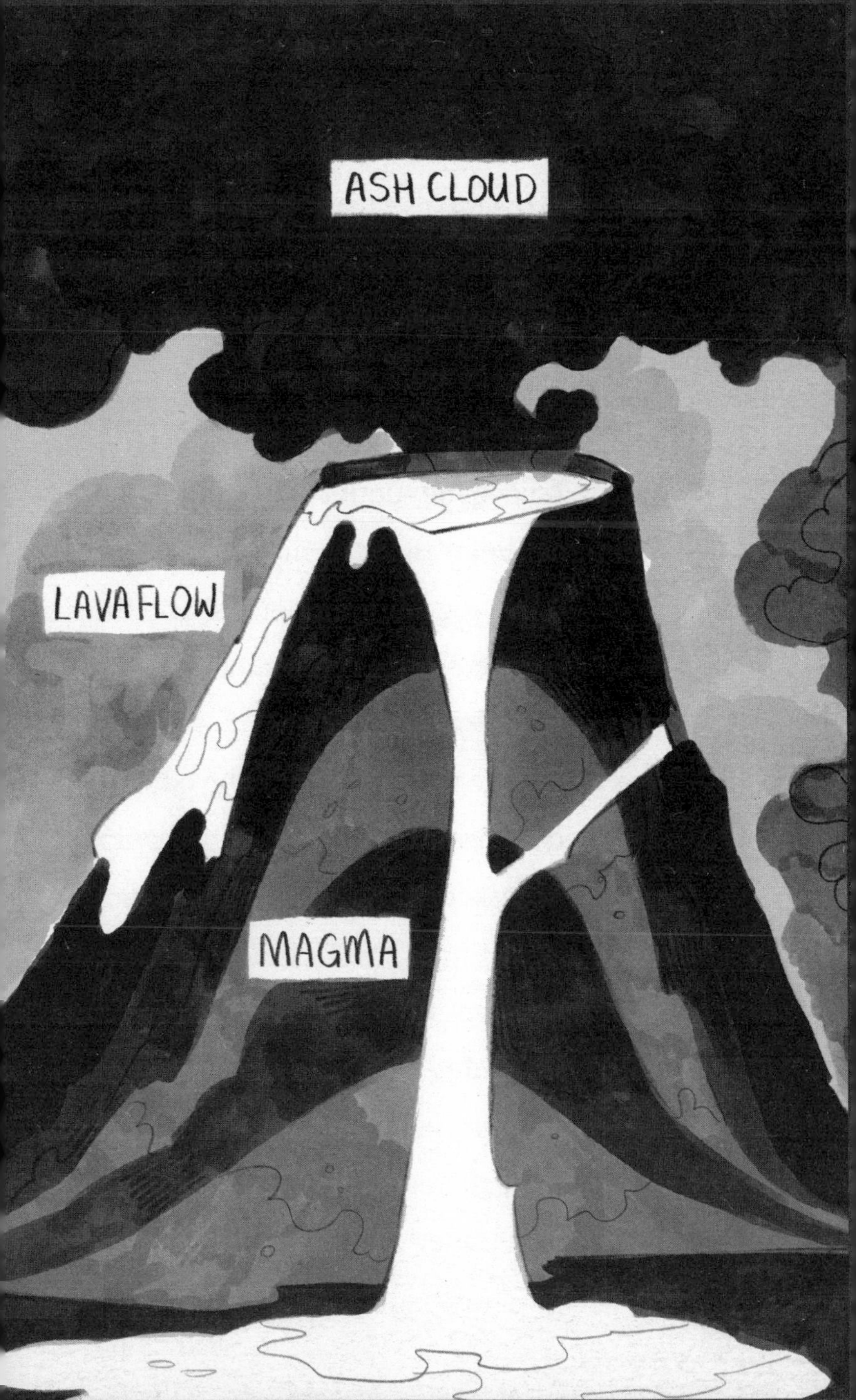
ASH CLOUD
LAVA FLOW
MAGMA

'Helga Sparks!' Dr Mizuki had her in her line of sight. 'Are you also teaching this class?'

For a moment, Olivia wondered where she had heard the name Sparks before, but she couldn't place it.

'No, Doctor Mizuki,' said Helga meekly.

'I mean, I have no doubt you could!' Dr Mizuki said, smiling. 'But it is my job, and we all need to learn together, so let's share the information. Please stand up and tell us what you know about volcanic eruptions.'

Relieved that she wasn't about to be chosen, Olivia looked more closely at Dr Mizuki. If she'd been asked to imagine a science teacher, she wouldn't have come up with Dr Mizuki with her **pink stripy hair**, nose ring and a blossoming flower tattooed on her left hand. Olivia wondered if the flower was one from the angel tree, but she couldn't see enough of it from under the cuff of Dr Mizuki's very bright green jumper.

'Volcanoes,' said Helga, standing up and brushing her fringe out of her eyes, 'form in places where the plates that cover the Earth's surface push together or move apart. This causes the mantle of the Earth to melt and makes a liquid rock called **lava,** which can move upwards through the weak point, or the volcano, to erupt from the Earth's surface, bringing water and gases with it.' She sat down, her face rather red.

'You're very clever.' Olivia was envious.

'And I'm very pretty,' said Ravi mischievously. 'So now you've got the two best people in the class as your friends.'

Olivia cheered up at the thought of having two friends!

'Well done, Helga!'

The rest of the class sighed. They didn't mind Helga being clever and knowing everything, especially as it made life a little easier for the rest of them. But, just sometimes, they did wish someone other than Helga would know the answer.

'Now,' said Dr Mizuki. 'Does anyone know which gases escape from a volcano?'

A small boy on the front row ventured a hand in the air as Helga was wrestling with herself not to raise her arm again.

'Oxygen?' he said shyly.

'Nice try, but no,' said Dr Mizuki. 'Anyone else?'

A tall girl at the back put her hand up. 'I don't know the name, but it smells really farty.'

The whole class **giggled**. Olivia tried to join in, but started too late so was still pretending to laugh when everyone else had stopped.

'Yes, Amari,' replied Dr Mizuki. 'The stinky egg gas – that's sulphur. It's one of the gases that can also come out when you do a fart. Sulphur dioxide does come out of volcanoes but there's one other gas that is the main gas I want to talk about.'

'**Poo-ee**.' Everyone held their noses.

'Princess Olivia is a fart,' whispered someone two rows behind Olivia. It wasn't loud enough for the teacher to hear, but Olivia heard it perfectly – as did Ravi and Helga, who turned round to glare fiercely behind her. Olivia shrank further into her seat.

'The answer,' said Dr Mizuki, 'is **carbon dioxide**. Volcanoes spew huge quantities of this gas into the Earth's atmosphere – and have been doing so for billions of years. In fact, without volcanoes, it is possible that the Earth would never have warmed enough for life to begin because carbon dioxide from volcanoes put **a warm blanket** round it. So, who can tell me – what is carbon dioxide? And what does it do?'

Olivia's ears pricked up and she tuned in

more carefully to what Dr Mizuki was saying. This sounded fascinating! But unfortunately, this also meant she caught Dr Mizuki's eye.

'Let's ask our newest student. Olivia, tell me, what is carbon dioxide and what does it do?'

Olivia decided her only option was to tell the truth. She took in a deep breath . . .

'**I don't know**,' she said. 'Because I used to live in a palace on top of a mountain, where I could only learn about things from really ancient books. And I never read about kar-bonne die-yoxide because the books were all about kings and queens and old fairy stories, and my tutors only taught me table manners and how to stand up straight with a heavy crown on my head. And you're all so clever,' she confessed. 'And I don't know *anything*.' Tears had started forming in her eyes so she stopped.

Ravi passed her a perfectly ironed hand-kerchief to wipe her eyes. But Olivia was embarrassed that she had given such a big display of emotions. She liked to do this in private normally.

'Ahhh,' the rest of the class said sadly, now wishing they hadn't been so unkind earlier.

'I don't even really know what science is,' Olivia added in a burst.

'Science,' said Dr Mizuki, 'is how we understand the world around us through theory, experiment and evidence. We look for rational explanations for why things are the way they are. People who do science are called **scientists** and it's their job to ask questions and find answers.'

Olivia's tears stopped abruptly.

'You mean, there really are reasons for things?' she cried. '**Ones we can work out and understand?**'

'Of course,' said Dr Mizuki.

'Like why trees have leaves and flowers, or

why clouds rain?' said Olivia, thinking of the huge angel tree she had seen such a long time ago with her dad.

'Yes, all that,' said Dr Mizuki. 'And the more we find out about the world around us, the more we can work out other, more complicated things, such as how the universe began or how life got started on Earth.'

'How *did* life get started on Earth?' said Helga keenly.

'We don't know,' said Dr Mizuki. 'Which is **exciting** because it means that one day one of you might grow up to become a scientist and find out!'

'If I became a scientist,' said Olivia slowly – her tears had dried up entirely now – 'could I try and work out why the **weather** has gone **wrong** in Alez?'

Dr Mizuki gave her a curious look. 'What do you mean, the weather has gone wrong?'

'Like you said about the volcanoes making the Earth warmer,' said Olivia, trying to piece her thoughts together. 'Because of a blanket round the Earth that changed everything. It feels like it's changing again – but why?'

Dr Mizuki nodded. 'It's an interesting point you make, Olivia. Carbon dioxide may once have been responsible for creating the right conditions on Earth for life, but now it might be having quite the **opposite** effect. Trees, for example, breathe in carbon dioxide and recycle it into the atmosphere as oxygen – which *we* then inhale and exhale as carbon dioxide. But the balance is being disturbed –' Suddenly Dr Mizuki seemed to pull herself up short and shuffled the papers on her desk.

'Well, I think that's enough for today!' she exclaimed brightly. 'Look! It's just about going-home time!'

At that moment, the bell rang for the end

of the school day. All the kids jumped up immediately and grabbed their bags, jostling for the exit. They were pushing so hard to get out that Olivia got swept up in the crowd and was nearly out of the door before she realized that she hadn't got proper answers to any of the questions she'd asked today. There was no way of fighting her way back into the classroom to ask Dr Mizuki, so Olivia made a note in her head to track the science teacher down and find out more as soon as she could.

CHAPTER 4

Paragona was waiting for Olivia when she emerged from school, arm in arm with Ravi and Helga. One of Helga's mums was there to greet her, but Ravi didn't seem to have anyone at all.

'Oh, I walk home alone,' he said cheerfully

to Paragona, who noticed him setting off by himself. 'My mum is at work so she can't meet me.'

'Which way are you going?' asked Paragona; she felt shocked to think of a child walking around alone in a kingdom that she and her husband used to rule. She put the thought aside to consider later.

Ravi pointed in the same direction that Olivia's family now lived, so the three of them wandered along together, through the dirty streets with the thick dark clouds overhead, Paragona minding her feet carefully.

'I must have a word with your father about this,' Paragona said crossly to Olivia, waving an imperious hand around to indicate everything in sight. 'It really is **dreadful**. He can put himself to good use and do something about it!'

Olivia doubted that. It wasn't just that he

was no longer king and so had no powers. Since they'd moved out of the palace and into the tiny apartment, her father had rarely got out of bed. That morning when she left for school was the first time for ages she'd seen the former King Tolemy upright and not wearing pyjamas. Or heard him speaking. He'd gone very silent since they had left the palace. Olivia thought he might have said more actual words that morning than he had in the whole time since they got on that ancient bus and left their old lives behind.

'How did you get on with the other children?' asked Paragona.

'Helga seemed to like me,' said Olivia thoughtfully.

'Who's Helga?' asked Paragona eagerly.

'You know,' said Olivia. 'The one who told you about the monarchy being a tool of oh-presh-shon.'

'Ah,' said Paragona, her face falling. Helga wasn't her idea of the perfect friend for her daughter. She seemed a bit too serious, not to mention all the backchat about royalty.

'Didn't you meet anyone more . . . noble?' she asked hopefully.

'Noble?' said Ravi. 'Well, there's me for a start!'

'You're . . . a . . .' Paragona couldn't finish the sentence, but she hadn't imagined that her daughter's first friend would be a boy who wore **butterfly wings**.

'I'm a princess in waiting,' he informed her gravely, fluttering his beautiful eyelashes.

Paragona widened her eyes in surprise but said nothing. At least someone wanted to be a princess, even if it wasn't her daughter.

'This is me!' Ravi sang in front of a tall,

decrepit-looking tower block whose top floors were hidden by the thick blanket of cloud which appeared to be coming downwards. 'Hurry home, the rain is coming – again!'

Back in the apartment, Olivia looked about at the huge furniture and ornaments crammed into the tiny space. A few days after they had left the palace, Paragona had been wandering about the streets in a daze, trying to get to know the city from this angle rather than looking down on it from the mountaintop palace, when she had spotted some of the royal family's old belongings thrown into a skip on the side of the road. Not the really beautiful things. Obviously Jeremy Pont liked *some* things about the royal family.

She and Tolemy had promptly rescued everything. Or rather Tolemy's twin brother, Olivia's favourite (and only) uncle, did. **Uncle Cassander** was as **practical and no-nonsense** as his identical twin was whimsical and distracted.

Cassander had left the palace years before. The rules of monarchy meant that even though he was only born **two minutes** after Tolemy, he was treated as a second-class citizen by everyone in the palace. Now Cassander lived on an island in the bay that bordered the port city of Alez. There he surfed, repaired old motorbikes and tried to forget he'd ever been a prince at all. He wasn't remotely upset about

Alez becoming a republic and not a kingdom – in fact, he thought it was high time the old ways were replaced.

But he was saddened by the impact this had on his family and how upset Tolemy and Paragona, whom he loved dearly, had become. When they had been rudely kicked out of the palace that morning, Cassander had heard the news and come over from his island to help them. It had been Cassander who had done all their paperwork to register them as ordinary citizens, to find them an apartment, Cassander who had reassured Olivia that everything really would be OK. Tolemy and Paragona had behaved like **frightened kittens** lost in a storm, whereas Cassander had been more like a comforting **Alsatian dog**, keeping them together and herding them to a place of safety.

As they climbed the stairs, the rain clearly getting fiercer by the sounds of it, Olivia thought that she would call her uncle to tell him about everything she'd learned today.

The radio news was playing as they entered the flat. '*And today, citizens of Alez,*' the newsreader enthused, '*we're going to be having more refreshing rain! Lucky us! Although it's raining, that doesn't mean we stop preparing for Day Zero! We need a lot more water to come, listeners, before we've got enough for everyone. And I've got a personal message here from our great leader, Jeremy! He says not to collect rainwater to drink! Don't do it, folks!* **Don't drink the rain!** *That's directly from the president himself!*'

Paragona angrily switched off the radio as Olivia's dad wandered into the sitting room. Olivia was delighted to see he was still out of bed! He *was* back in his pyjamas and his velvet dressing gown, which had a crown embroidered on the jacket pocket, and he was wearing his slippers with the royal motif all over them. But, thought Olivia, at least he was awake. Tolemy

tended to spend the whole day asleep and then wander around the tiny flat noisily at night.

'How's my favourite princess?' he beamed, **holding out his arms for a hug** as Olivia ran to him. She was so happy to see him smile she didn't even correct him when he called her a princess. 'How was your first day at school?'

Olivia thought for a moment and rearranged her glasses, which had gone askew from her dad's bear hug. She didn't want to lie to her parents, but she remembered the tome she'd read on diplomacy in the palace library and how it had said that in certain circumstances, it was better to tell a happy fiction rather than a painful truth.

'It was great,' she said. 'And I've got a message for you – it's *bottled or boiled*!'

'What?' asked her dad.

'We can't drink water from the tap,' explained Olivia.

'What are we meant to drink?' said Paragona in bewilderment.

'We have to drink bottled water or boil it,' said Olivia. 'And no baths!'

Paragona looked appalled. 'So now we have to be thirsty and smelly as well as everything else!'

'I don't understand,' said the former king. 'The water in Alez comes from the glacier. At least, it did to the palace. I don't know what happened in the rest of the country . . .' He trailed off.

'People drinking rainwater!' said her mother, thinking of the radio report. 'Whatever next!'

As it happened, Olivia was ready to tell her what was coming next.

'**I want to be a scientist**,' she proclaimed.

Her mother gasped.

'A scientist!' said her dad. 'That's an amazing idea! But . . . what do scientists actually do?'

'A scientist is a person who finds out the reasons for why things are the way they are,' said Olivia.

'*A scientist!*' echoed Paragona, wondering by now whether this endless day would just keep on surprising her right up until bedtime. 'You can't be a scientist!'

'Why not?' said Olivia, who until now had always said she wanted to be a detective.

'Scientists are all men,' said Paragona firmly, as though that settled it.

'Dr Mizuki is a scientist,' retorted Olivia.

'You'll have to wear a white coat and live in a

laboratory,' said Paragona threateningly.

'**Fantastic!**' said Olivia gleefully, thinking that would mean no more party dresses or uncomfortable shoes. 'And I'll be able to find out the answers to all sorts of important questions!'

'Questions!' said Tolemy. '**What kind of questions?**' In his whole life he had never asked an important question, even if he'd wanted to. Kings were supposed to know everything, so he had always pretended he had.

'Like, why can't we drink the water?' said Olivia. 'Or why is the water running out? Why are the clouds all brown and dirty? And why is it always too hot? Or too cold? Those kinds of things. Don't you think we need to know?'

'I didn't know any of those things were happening. I think we *do* need to know!' Tolemy had a rare burst of enthusiasm. 'But first – what's for tea?! Is that a question my clever scientist can answer?' He hugged his daughter again and she was so delighted that she decided not to mention science again. At least, not today.

But that didn't mean she couldn't think about it, and come up with some new questions of her own. Her map book from the palace was sitting on the kitchen table as she followed her parents into the little kitchenette, where they struggled to make a meal from the few raw ingredients they were able to buy. Olivia snatched up the book and held it close. A thought went through her head – it was time to make **a new map** of Alez.

CHAPTER 5

The next day, Olivia made her mother get ready to leave home much earlier, and insisted that she wore a pair of sensible shoes. This was more complicated than it should have been as it turned out Paragona didn't have any shoes she could walk very far in.

She had lots of amazing high heels, beautiful handmade boots and strappy sandals. But nothing that counted as practical. In the end, Olivia persuaded her mother to wear a pair of her old sneakers that she didn't wear anymore, to walk to school in.

Olivia felt more confident when she saw Ravi standing by the gate waiting for her, and fortunately Paragona was so mortified about her shabby shoes that she was quite happy to leave Olivia and hurry away before she was spotted by any of the other parents.

A **big sign** hanging on the school gate read:

SMOG ALERT!
Sports and outside break
time cancelled today.

'Olly! No crown?' said Ravi, looking disappointed at Olivia's outfit.

'No,' said Olivia darkly. 'I won't be wearing it again.'

'Can I wear it one day?' asked Ravi, hopefully. Today he had a pair of angel wings pinned to his jumper and a skirt over his trousers.

'You can have it,' said Olivia. 'Forever. What's smog?' She pointed to the same notice, this one pinned on the school door.

'It's the **dirty air**,' said Ravi.

'Where does it come from?' asked Olivia. 'And what's it made of?'

Ravi looked surprised. 'Well, I don't know,' he said. 'I just thought this was how everywhere was.'

'Not up at the palace it wasn't!' said Olivia, remembering the clear air and sparkling sunshine at the mountaintop.

'**We can't all live in a palace**,' said Helga,

who had sneaked up behind them.

'I wish we could,' said Ravi. 'Think of the jewels!'

'**Don't be silly!**' exclaimed Olivia. 'I don't live in a palace any more! But because I did, I know it's different down here in the city. But we don't know why, and I think we should ask the question. Y'know, like Doctor Mizuki said, be like scientists!'

'You want to be a scientist?' Helga said. 'You didn't even know what science was yesterday!'

'Now I do,' said Olivia, a little haughtily. 'I was going to be a detective but then school turned out not to be like it is in the books and I think there are more mysteries in finding out about the world. So now I want to be a scientist.'

A terrible thought struck her. Helga was so clever and knowledgeable. Was she going to be a scientist too? Was there a limit on how many people could become scientists? If it came to a choice between her and Helga, she was quite sure Helga would win hands down.

'I'm going to be **President of Alez**,' said Helga, as though she had read Olivia's mind.

'Are you?' laughed Ravi. 'And how are you going to do that?'

'I haven't figured out my plan in detail,' Helga confessed seriously, as they settled into the same desks as yesterday. 'But my mums say this country was left in **an appalling mess** by a parasite monarchy – ouch!' She looked accusingly at Ravi, who had pinched her forearm. 'I mean, I'm working on it.' She hastily changed the subject, getting out what looked like a thin black shiny book with a silver back. It looked beautiful and mysterious, like nothing Olivia had seen before. Suddenly she desperately wanted one for herself.

'Have your mums said anything about the

weather?' she asked Helga, suddenly wondering if Helga's two mothers, who seemed to know about everything, might help her understand.

Helga looked perplexed for a moment. 'No,' she said slowly. 'I don't think they have. That's strange . . . they are always talking about making daily life better for ordinary people, but not about –' Helga changed tack. 'How are you going to become a scientist?'

'I don't yet know,' said Olivia.

'You need a plan,' said Ravi, also getting a similar flat black book-shaped thing out of his backpack.

'**What is that?**' said Olivia, pointing at it.

'Excuse me?' said Ravi in astonishment. 'You don't know what an iPad is? Even one as old as this?'

'An eye pad?' said Olivia, wondering if it had something to do with the cold compresses that her mother used to wear when she was lying on

her bed after some horrible breach of protocol had given her a headache.

'You have heard of **the internet**, haven't you?' said Helga from behind her.

'Erm . . .' Olivia didn't want to admit that she had not.

'Mind you, the school network is pretty bad,' Helga carried on in what Olivia realized was her usual way of being unable to say one thing when she could say three. 'They block lots of sites so we can't really find out anything useful.'

'It's the same at home!' said Ravi. 'It's not just school! There's a **block** now on anything we might really want to know about! It wasn't always like that. Here.' Ravi handed his iPad to Olivia. 'It's like a computerized book, except you can also find out stuff or do shopping, or watch cartoons or the news. Although I don't think the news is really that true . . .'

'Can I find out what kar-bonne die-yoxide is?' asked Olivia. Her parents hadn't had the foggiest when she'd asked them the night before. And Uncle Cassander hadn't answered the phone when she'd tried to call him. Her mother had thought that kar-bonne might have a distant relationship to diamonds, which had then reminded her to check that her collection of crowns and tiaras was still hidden inside the old pillowcase, and then she'd been distracted for hours. Her father had vaguely muttered something about pencils. But Olivia felt pretty sure that neither diamonds nor pencils spewed out of the top of volcanoes and weren't formed in the air from gases, so she had got no further.

'Sure,' said Ravi. He typed 'carbon dioxide' into the browser while Olivia made a mental note of the spelling.

A page appeared on the screen. Olivia gasped!

'**That's magic!**' she breathed.

'No, Olly, it isn't,' said Helga severely. 'It's digitalized communication, which is not the same thing at all. You'll need to know that if you're going to be a scientist.'

Carbon dioxide, read the page, is a chemical compound made of one carbon atom joined with two oxygen atoms. It is present in the Earth's atmosphere from natural causes such as volcanic eruptions or biological processes. Carbon dioxide is also known as a greenhouse ...

But there the print went squiggly and Olivia couldn't read it.

'I think there's something wrong with your eye pad,' she said to Ravi. 'Look!' She pointed to the next sentence, which started:

Carbon dioxide in large concentrations can be harmful to weather, human and animal health and the oceans because

But after the word 'because', it was completely unreadable. Further down, it said:

Produced in damagingly large quantities through – but again the rest of the sentence had been made **impossible to read**, as though it had suddenly turned into a row of Egyptian hieroglyphs.

'I don't understand,' said Olivia in bemusement. 'Why can't I read it?'

'You were looking for something to

investigate,' said Ravi. 'Looks like you just found it.'

'I have!' said Olivia. 'And the question is – why does Alez not look the way it did? And **why isn't anyone talking about it?** Here, look at my book! It's a real book, not a computer book, but that means it's got things in it we can actually see and read.'

She produced the old book out of her bag, happy to have something she could show her friends.

'See!' She showed them the pages of the book where every corner of the former kingdom was pictured either in brilliant shades of paint, or in photos, showing a clean, fertile country with blue rivers, green trees, animals, birds and butterflies living alongside tiny farms and snug hamlets.

'Is that really Alez City?' said Ravi, pointing at the picture showing a wide blue bay where

dolphins jumped out of the cresting waves and fishers with small boats cast their nets into clear water. 'It's **underwater** there now! And it's grey and muddy!'

'What about this!' said Helga, pointing at a picture of a park in the centre of the city with a huge tree in the middle.

'What's that tree?' said Ravi curiously.

Olivia looked more closely, and her heart skipped a beat.

'It's an angel tree!' she said. 'I didn't know there was one in the city too!'

'Never heard of it,' said Ravi, wrinkling his nose.

'You've **never heard** of the **angel tree?**' said Olivia, who couldn't believe this. 'It's the symbol of Alez! It keeps us safe!'

'Hasn't done a great job so far,' said Ravi, peering at the picture.

'That tree isn't there any more!' said Helga.

'I know that park! There's nothing left.'

Adanna had snuck up behind them and was looking at Olivia's book over her shoulder. 'Is that your house?' she asked, amazed, pointing to an old photo of the palace.

'Yes,' said Olivia, sighing a little, wondering why that made her feel sad. 'Well – my old house . . .'

'What's that funny thing at the side?' Adanna asked.

'It's a **greenhouse**,' said Olivia.

'What's it for?' said Ravi. 'It looks like a playhouse made of glass. That's weird.'

'It's to keep things warm,' explained Olivia. 'The gardeners grew tomatoes and peppers in it.'

'Oh, very posh,' exclaimed Helga. 'The **royal tomato!**'

'Not really,' said Olivia matter-of-factly. 'It was for growing stuff that would be too cold outside.'

'It's not too cold now,' pointed out Ravi.

'Exactly!' said Olivia. 'That's why we need to investigate!'

'How are we going to do that?' asked Ravi.

'We're going to use science to solve the mystery of the weather! It's **the most important problem we could solve**. And we have to do it ourselves because Mr V won't tell us, Dr Mizuki didn't answer, and now the internet doesn't want us to read about it!'

'Ooh,' said Ravi. 'What shall we call ourselves? If we're going to solve a science mystery, we need a secret name!'

'How about . . .' said Helga. 'HRO!'

'What?' said Ravi.

'Helga Ravi Olivia!' said Helga proudly. 'It's our names!'

'Why are you first?' grumbled Ravi. 'It wasn't your idea to have a name. It should be RHO!'

'What about ARHO?' said Adanna.

'Adanna!' said Helga. 'There are only **three people in this club**! It's super-exclusive and you have to be invited to join.'

Adanna sidled away, looking hurt.

'What?' said Helga, seeing the other two give her a look. 'We can't let everyone join! We'll never get anything done.'

'I think it's got to have the word "investigation" in it!' said Olivia.

'Spot on!' said Ravi, still thinking. 'Let's be ORHI! It's our names but it also stands for . . . Office of Royal High Investigations?' he said excitedly.

'No!' said Olivia, feeling she had quite enough things in her home life that had royal titles given them by her parents – such as the royal toaster, the royal bath towel, the royal egg cup. 'And anyway, someone's trying to stop us from finding out what's really going on, so we need to call it the Office of *Real* High

Investigations!'

'**Brilliant!**' said Helga, whose usually pale cheeks were quite flushed now. 'Bags I be **president!**'

The group now known as ORHI settled into their seats as the bell went for the first lesson.

Dr Mizuki stormed in, looking rather cross. Olivia put her hand up straight away to ask her question from yesterday. But Dr Mizuki snapped at her, 'Olivia, put your hand down! I'll tell you when it's time to ask questions.'

'But,' said Olivia, tilting her chin in a determined manner. 'You said –'

'Today's topic!' said Dr Mizuki firmly, cutting Olivia off completely, 'is **investigation**! How do we investigate a topic from a scientific viewpoint?'

The ORHI group nudged each other excitedly. Olivia thought she saw Dr Mizuki give her a flicker of a smile, even though it vanished so fast she couldn't be sure she'd seen it. She wondered what was going on.

'Where do we start in trying to understand the world around us through science?' said Dr Mizuki.

At the back, a couple of children wheezed and puffed on their inhalers.

Helga put her hand up. But it didn't seem as though Dr Mizuki wanted to be interactive at

all today. She didn't wait to gather any answers to her questions and carried on speaking.

'We make an **observation!** This can be something from around us that we are experiencing, seeing or even smelling!' She wrote the word 'observation' in big letters on the whiteboard.

A forest of hands went up with suggestions. Dr Mizuki picked a few students, pointedly avoiding Olivia and her new friends, now sitting together in the front row.

'Some things float, and some things sink!' said one child excitedly.

'I won't ask what inspired that question,' said Dr Mizuki drily.

'That tree is dying!' shouted another, pointing to a tree outside the classroom window. Olivia peered out of the window and saw a tree that might once even have been an angel tree; it was impossible to know now because it had only bare branches against the orange-grey sky.

'The weather is changing!' yelled Ravi, deciding to join in. The ORHI group sat up to attention and waited for a reaction which didn't come.

Dr Mizuki ploughed determinedly onwards. The ORHI exchanged significant glances with each other.

'And then we ask ourselves a question about our observation! It could be "What things float in water and what sinks?" Moving on, we then **form a hypothesis!**' continued Dr Mizuki, writing it on the board. 'This could be something that starts with "I think" and could be your version of an explanation for what you have noticed and asked your question about. We could say, "I think that dense things sink, and light things float in water", for example.'

Olivia wrote down the word 'hypothesis' in her notebook and underlined it several times.

'Then,' said Dr Mizuki, writing on the board again, 'we think of a way to test your hypothesis by designing an *experiment*. We record **our results** and discuss them to find out what we learned! Is everyone clear?'

Helga, Ravi and Olivia all had their hands in the air, waving madly. But Dr Mizuki just blanked them again.

'Good!' she said. 'In that case, I've got an experiment for you! We're going to show that heat rises.'

'Heat rises?' the ORHI group mouthed to each other in confusion. The rest of the class looked baffled. This didn't match up with any of the suggestions they had made.

But Olivia, as she watched Dr Mizuki get out a row of glass jars and put food colouring into them and then hurry away to find some hot water, realized this might just be **another clue** that could help them.

Heat rises, thought Olivia, writing in her book. A thought came into her mind as she remembered again the greenhouse at the palace with its fruity smells of warm damp earth and its huge leafy palms in the humid warm air. She also remembered the half-line on the internet that read 'carbon dioxide is a greenhouse . . .'

She drew a little picture of the greenhouse in her notebook and put arrows to show the heat going upwards inside. She remembered that going into the greenhouse felt like being **wrapped in a hot wet towel**, even when there was snow on the ground outside. *It means something*, she said to herself. *But I don't know what . . .*

At break time, Olivia didn't sit with Ravi and Helga in the classroom, where the students had to stay today because the air was too bad for them to play outside. *Smog*, she reminded herself. Instead, she made an excuse and went to find the hub, which her new friends had told her was where the teachers spent their precious free minutes out of the classroom.

SMOG
by Mira Adhikari

If you live in a city that has a lot of factories and cars, you might have noticed the sky looking hazy and brown some days, making it difficult to see. This is called smog, and it is what we call air pollution when it gets very bad and reduces our visibility.

Smog is a mixture of two words: smoke and fog. It is made up of lots of different pollutants, which come from car exhausts, coal power plants, and man-made chemicals. When the Sun's rays react with these pollutants they can form a gas called ozone. The pollutants can also include tiny particles, which are responsible for the sky looking brown and making it hard to see. This combination of ozone and tiny particles is what makes up smog.

Ozone that is naturally present high up in our atmosphere actually protects us from the harmful effects of the Sun's rays, but if ozone is formed near the ground and close to us, it can cause lots of health problems. Ozone and the tiny particles may not always be visible in the air but can be dangerous for our heart and lungs and make breathing difficult. It can also irritate the eyes and nose and make them itchy. Smog has harmful effects on plants and animals as well, so it's important that we try and limit the amount of pollutants we produce.

Olivia found a door that had STAFF ROOM written on it and knocked. Mr V answered and smiled when he saw his newest student. 'Olivia,' he said. 'Is everything OK?'

'Yes!' said Olivia. 'Or . . . no . . . I'm not sure.' She felt confused.

'Olivia,' said Mr V. 'You can talk to me any time. So much change must be difficult for you. How is everything at home?'

'It's fine!' said Olivia quickly, but she felt tears forming in her eyes again. She pushed them away. 'Everything is great at home and at school!'

'Really?' said Mr V. 'You've been through some very big changes in your life. It can't be easy for you. Or your parents.'

'It is easy,' said Olivia firmly. 'And I'm completely OK. I always wanted to go to school, and I never wanted to be a princess, so it's all going really well for me.' She was surprised to find her voice turned into a funny croak by the end of the sentence.

'Aha,' said Mr V nicely, leaning on the doorframe. 'Shall we make a proper time to talk things through? **Feelings** are **important**, Olivia. It matters that you take note of how you feel and find someone to talk to.'

'There are things I want to talk about now. That's why I'm here,' said Olivia, who was determined not to cry again. 'But not about *feelings*. I have lots of questions. I want to talk about the weather!'

'The weather?' Now Mr V was the one sounding confused. 'Why do you want to talk about the weather? Do your emotions make you think of stormy days, and you want to feel as though the Sun is shining again?'

'Yes,' said Olivia. 'I mean, you can't picnic in the rain, so of course I like sunshine best.'

At that moment, Olivia saw the bright pink hair of Dr Mizuki coming towards them. But when the science teacher saw Olivia talking to Mr V, she suddenly seemed to remember something urgent and set off running in the opposite direction.

'Doctor Mizuki!' Olivia called after her hopefully. 'Can we talk about the weather? And greenhouses?' But it was too late; the science teacher had vanished round the corner. Olivia had the definite impression that Dr Mizuki was **avoiding** her.

'So, feelings?' said Mr V optimistically. 'Would now be a good time to talk about feelings?'

'No!' said Olivia crossly. 'I need to go and write down what Dr Mizuki just told us in class about experiments! That's **way more important** than stupid feelings!'

CHAPTER 6

At home that evening, gazing out of the window, Olivia thought about what had happened that day. Outside, the clouds were boiling in the sky, dropping a monsoon of rain which was falling so hard and fast it made rivers of the roads and swept all the rubbish along with it. There were bicycles, umbrellas, food wrappers, toys, plastic bottles – and **even a sofa** – sailing down the street below, heading for the sea.

Olivia hoped she and her family were safe, up high in their tower block. She looked up, spooked, as the electricity in the apartment flickered a few times and went off – but it came back on a moment later. She shivered. Whatever was happening in Alez, it seemed to be **getting worse** by the day.

She couldn't bear to watch the weather any more, so instead she got out her special notebook from Uncle Cassander and sat her bear – now renamed Citizen George in line with the new family status – next to her. The notebook had a code to lock it, which was very useful as she had more than once suspected her parents of snooping when she was out at school. She entered her code – which was not her birthday as she knew that would be the first one her mother would try – and opened it up. Olivia had quite a bit to think about and she always found that writing down her thoughts helped her to organize her head. With that in mind, she picked up her pencil and wrote:

Office of Real High Investigations

Investigation One – The Wrong Weather

QUESTION: What has gone wrong with the weather? Why can't I find out any information about it on the internet? Why won't the teachers answer my questions?

What is the evidence?

• Carbon dioxide puts a warm blanket round the Earth – but where is it coming from? Trees

breathe carbon dioxide, which takes it out of the air. Have the trees stopped breathing?
• Heat rises - but what does that mean? Why doesn't it just go away?

Greenhouses?

HYPOTHESIS: I think Alez is getting warmer. This is making the weather go weird and that is doing all sorts of other things to the world we live in.

PREDICTION: If it doesn't stop, things will get way worse.

TEST THE PREDICTION: Stop it happening and see if future Alez becomes a nicer place to live!!

CONCLUSION: If I can find this out, maybe Mum will feel happier because she thinks I need to do my royal duty as the future of Alez. And she won't cry all the time, and maybe Dad will stop sleeping all day. And I can be a scientist!

'Phew!' Olivia put down her pencil and exchanged glances with Citizen George. 'We need to talk to Uncle Cassander,' she told her bear. 'He's the **only one** who ever tells me the truth.'

Carefully, she tapped the number into the phone, which was so old it didn't have a touch pad, but numbered buttons instead, and waited as the line clicked through and rang a few times.

'Yello!' sang a cheerful voice, very loudly.

Olivia started and covered the receiver with her hand. 'Hello,' she whispered into the mouthpiece.

'Princess Olivia!' the voice said back, very loudly again.

'**Shhhh!**' said Olivia crossly. She didn't want her parents to know she was being a science detective. 'No, it's not!'

'Well, it sounds like Princess Olivia!' said the cheery voice, matching her in quietness this time.

'It's **just Olivia**,' said Olivia. 'You know **I'm not** a princess!'

'Habit! Olly, how are you?'

Olivia beamed into the phone. 'How are the

kittens?' she said longingly. Last time she had
seen her Uncle Cassander, he had shown her
pictures of the two adorable grey kittens he had
found on the beach one morning, looking as
though they needed a home.

'Still not surfing,' Uncle Cassander said with
pretend sadness. 'I don't understand it! I've
explained to them how fun it is.'

'You're so silly,' said Olivia, giggling. 'You
know cats don't like water!'

'I live in hope,' said Uncle Cassander. 'Now, my favourite and only niece. How can I **help** you?'

'Are there any volcanoes in Alez?' asked Olivia.

'**Oh!**' said Cassander in surprise. Whatever he thought Olivia was going to ask him, this certainly wasn't it. '**No, I don't think so**. Why?'

'Volcanoes,' said Olivia, 'send loads of something called carbon dioxide into the atmosphere when they erupt. And when the Earth was just a new baby planet, carbon dioxide helped it get warm enough for life to begin! Did you know that?'

'Er, maybe,' said Cassander. 'Or not. Why are you asking?'

'Because,' continued Olivia, 'Alez isn't like the pictures in my books. The weather has gone very wrong.'

'Yes,' said Cassander thoughtfully. 'There

have been a lot of storms across the bay! I haven't been able to cross over to the city for a few weeks now. And I have to keep moving my hut back because **the island** is getting **smaller and smaller**. What do you think is going on?'

'Well,' said Olivia importantly, 'I've got a hypothesis.'

'A hypo-what?' said Cassander in astonishment. Olivia felt surprised he didn't know. He'd always seemed so much more knowledgeable than her parents.

'It's an explanation based on some evidence which means you have to investigate,' said Olivia importantly.

'I see,' said Cassander.

'So, as I'm going to be a scientist –'

'You're going to be a scientist?' exclaimed Cassander. 'I thought you were going to be a police detective!'

'A scientist is a sort of detective,' said

Olivia. 'But instead of solving crimes, you try and solve puzzles about the natural world. It's way more interesting . . .'

'Tell me about your hypothesis, then.' Uncle Cassander was intrigued.

'OK,' said Olivia. 'Here it is. I think . . . **something** is **changing the world** we live in, not in a good way. And I think it's got something to do with stuff going into the atmosphere that is changing the temperature, just like the Earth warmed millions of years ago. I thought it might be coming from volcanoes, but if there aren't any in Alez, then it's got to be something else. What? And why is it happening now? And what's it got to do with greenhouses?'

'Now you mention it,' said Cassander, 'I've noticed that the ocean is much warmer than it used to be. And the storms are getting bigger and closer to the shore.'

'Oh!' said Olivia, thinking this sounded important.

But before Cassander could say anything more, Paragona burst into the hallway and grabbed the phone from Olivia.

'Cassander!' she cried into the phone. 'Is that you?'

Olivia was shooed away to her room and after that could only hear half the conversation,

and she didn't really need to listen because she'd heard it many times already – about how much her parents hated their new life and wanted to go back to the palace and be the king and queen again.

Her mother appeared at the door and gave Olivia what was the closest to a smile she had seen for some time.

'Your **Uncle Cassander** is **coming to stay!**' she announced. 'It's just what your father needs!'

Olivia doubted that was strictly true – Tolemy and Cassander didn't really get on that well, but Olivia felt that anything would be better than the heavy gloom in the tiny apartment – which her mother had renamed the Royal Residence – than they had at the moment.

Grown-ups, Olivia reflected, were really good at being sad about pointless things that they couldn't change, and staying sad for a ridiculously long time. She resolved that when she was a grown-up, she would never be sad about anything and would just get on and solve mysteries using the power of science if she ever needed to cheer herself up. As for feelings – she allowed herself a little snort in the manner, she hoped, of the grande marquessa – they would just have to wait until she'd solved the mystery of why the weather had gone so very wrong.

CHAPTER 7

Olivia had called a meeting of ORHI. They had tried to hold it at school, but the other kids kept nosing in on what they were doing. Despite her bad start, Olivia had somehow gained a fan base, which meant the ORHI group never got a moment alone. Every moment, someone would sidle up and ask Olivia questions about her former life or what the palace was really like or whether she had any royal stuff they could borrow for dressing up.

Ravi told them he didn't think ORHI should meet at his place because his mum would insist on feeding them all, and they already didn't have enough food for themselves (the vegetables on his balcony weren't growing very well in the weird weather).

Olivia noted this down in her code-locked notebook too – this was another surprise for her about the new Alez, how difficult it was for everyone to get food. At the palace, there was **so much to eat** that every evening the cooks would **throw out** huge piles of **perfectly good dishes** that no one wanted. Olivia wondered if she could go back to the palace and ask them for all the thrown-away food so she could take it around Alez City and give it to people without enough to eat, which on some days included her and her parents. She marked it down as a plan for when she had solved her first mystery.

At the same time, Olivia certainly didn't think she could offer to hold the meeting at the new-style 'Royal Residence'.

Her dad would be asleep in the middle of the afternoon, which would be hard to explain to the others. As for Paragona, she would be unlikely to leave them alone for a second, and Olivia also suspected that Ravi wouldn't concentrate on what she had to say because he would get distracted by Paragona parading her collection of crowns and tiaras. And she was sure that Helga and her mother wouldn't get along very well, especially if Helga decided to lecture Paragona again – or the other way round!

Instead, after school, the two friends followed

Helga to her home, which turned out to be quite a long walk in the opposite direction from where Olivia and Ravi lived. They took **a steep uphill path** which Olivia soon realized led in the same direction as to the real palace. She sighed sadly at the thought of her old home, which she never believed she would miss so much. As they puffed upwards along the sharply rising stone steps, a thought struck Olivia.

'Are your mums OK about us coming round?' she called to Helga, who was far in front.

'Yes, of course!' Helga said, turning back and waiting for them. They were climbing into the cloud now, which hung over the port city. 'My mums will be at work anyway. My nanny will be home.'

'You've got a nanny?' said Ravi in disbelief. He had scaled the steps without stopping and didn't even seem to be out of breath.

'Er, yes,' said Helga, sounding embarrassed – Olivia didn't understand why; she had loved Nina, her nanny at the palace. 'Both my mums work all the time.'

Olivia's small legs had been struggling with the big steps. She caught up with Helga and Ravi, who were standing on a rock, looking out across the city below and the bay, just visible in its misty outline.

'I didn't know you lived up here!' said Ravi. 'I thought you lived **by the shipyard?**'

'I did,' said Helga matter-of-factly. 'But we

moved. When **the sea level rose**.' Olivia remembered Uncle Cassander saying he had to keep moving his hut as the sea came closer while the water got warmer. She wondered if this was the same thing. 'Mum and Mama saw that we would be underwater quite soon, so they looked for a place for us to live **on higher ground**. It's closer for them to get to work too.'

ON THE RISE: SEA LEVELS

by Dr Isabel Fendley

The height of the water in oceans around the world is known as the sea level. This level is also used as a starting measure of the elevation (height) of any place where the oceans touch land – the beaches and coastlines.

Global warming leads to sea-level rise in multiple ways. When glaciers and ice sheets on land melt, the water they produce is added to the ocean and so the sea level goes up, just like filling a bathtub. Also, the water in the oceans expands as the Earth warms, making sea levels rise even more.

When the sea level goes up, the edge of the ocean moves further on to land. As a result, sea-level rise affects all coastal regions around the world where the elevation is very close to sea level. As more ice melts, the sea level will get higher and higher and land near the coasts will begin to flood more often and more severely. For every 2 centimetres of sea-level rise, 1–2 metres more of beach are covered by the ocean – so even small amounts of sea-level rise can have a large effect on the lives of people who live near the coast.

'Where do your mums work?' asked Olivia. She had never heard of two parents working. Or even one, for that matter.

'At the government!' said Helga in surprise. 'I thought everyone knew that!'

'You mean, at the palace?' exclaimed Ravi. 'Like, **in Olivia's old home?**'

'Well, yes,' said Helga. 'I suppose they do now.' Helga looked over at Olivia. 'My mum didn't mean it, you know, Olly.'

'Mean what?' said Olivia. She had a little jolt of memory of Dr Mizuki talking to Helga. 'Sparks!' she said, quivering at the thought of that embarrassing and sad last day at the palace. 'Was that your mum?' she exclaimed, remembering the woman in the two-piece dark outfit who had helped Paragona out of the throne and then told them to leave. A name came back to her: 'Gretchen Sparks.'

'Yeah,' said Helga. 'She's the deputy

president! And Mama runs all the hospitals in Alez now.'

Olivia felt hot suddenly and her cheeks flushed. 'Your mum made my parents cry!' she burst out. 'She made us leave our house! And now she's going there every day! To our palace! **That's not fair!**'

'It was never about *you*,' said Helga stiffly.

'They were trying to do the right thing for Alez.'

Olivia looked out over the bay of Alez. The mist swirling in the wind made it hard to see the city clearly. But she could still make out the miles of tower blocks, the rusting ships in the harbour and the open spaces that once had been parks but had now turned into wastelands. She looked upwards, towards the palace, and realized she could just see the outlines of the sweeping walls in the distance and a shred of blue sky hanging above what once had been her home.

She felt too overwhelmed by her emotions to speak. **Why** hadn't she and her parents done a **better job** with Alez? Did her parents know it was in trouble and just not do anything about it? Could they have made it nicer? At least they should have been allowed to try. Would they ever get the chance again?

Ravi quickly realized that, like his friends,

the weather was brewing up for a storm. A curtain of dark cloud had fallen over half the sky while the other half was lit by sunshine that seemed too bright to be real. The sea was frothing as huge waves tumbled out in the bay. Far away, near the horizon, glowing lightning forked down to touch the water. A far-distant rumble told them that thunder was coming closer as raindrops splatted down on their heads.

'**C'mon!**' Ravi carolled. '**Race you there!**'

They pelted after him towards a gracious white house surrounded by trees, which surprised Olivia. She thought about the city where all the trees had died or been cut down. She stopped for a moment in a big porch with columns either side to wonder if she'd been there before, perhaps for a party when she was very little. Whoever lived there then, she knew it hadn't been Helga and her two mums. More likely some fancy duke and duchess, maybe even one of her relatives. Olivia wondered where they were now.

Once inside the huge front doors, Ravi and Olivia dripped across the marble floor, following Helga into what turned out to be a massive kitchen with a huge stove and a big wooden table in the middle. With the hood of her anorak over her head, Olivia's face couldn't be seen at all.

'I'm **soaked!**' crowed Ravi, taking off his coat and, from under that, his drenched wings. At that moment, a sweet-faced woman with long dark hair swept up in a large bun came rushing over.

'Oh, you poor children!' she cried. 'Helga, go and change in your room and I'll get towels and dry clothes for your friends!' She bustled out and reappeared from a side room with a heap of fluffy towels and a folded pile of clean T-shirts and pyjama trousers. But then suddenly she spied Olivia who had pushed her hood from her face and taken off her glasses.

'Princess Olivia!' the woman cried out.

Without her glasses, Olivia couldn't see who it was, but she knew the voice so well that she blundered blindly towards the speaker, ending up in a **giant hug**.

'Nina!' Olivia sobbed into her former nanny's shoulder. It was her ex-nanny! 'Nina! **I've missed you so much!**'

'Princess!' exclaimed Nina, holding her tight. 'How are you? How are your mum and dad?'

Olivia shook her

head miserably. 'Dad stays in bed and Mum just sits around, polishing her jewels,' she said gloomily.

'Oh dear,' said Nina. 'I'm so sorry for your family!'

'Why are you here?' asked Olivia, looking around, suddenly realizing how astonishing it was to see Nina again but in a completely different place.

'I look after Helga and her brother now,' said Nina. 'They're lovely children, very serious, very clever.' She grabbed a towel and rubbed Olivia's hair, in the way she had when she was very small.

'Do you ever go to the palace?' asked Olivia eagerly, from inside the towel. 'Is it very different now?'

Nina shook her head. 'It's **just the same** as it was before!' she whispered. 'They said they were going to make big changes to everything

– and it's just the same! Even the thrones are still there! And that man, that Jeremy, he sits on your dad's throne and pretends to be a king! But he's nothing like your father, who was always so polite and kind.'

'Is it still **clean and beautiful** at the palace?' whispered Olivia. 'Because it isn't in the city!'

'Yes!' said Nina. 'Up there, you wouldn't know anything was wrong! Even here, it's completely different.' She gently dried Olivia's face with the cloth and replaced her glasses.

'Because you can't **see** anything from the palace,' said Olivia slowly, working it out in her head. 'So **everything** looks **perfect!**'

Nina nodded. 'They can't see the outside world, just the way your parents couldn't.' Their eyes both turned to the big kitchen windows where the view of the garden had suddenly darkened as the treetops swirled in the vicious wind. Ravi, who had changed into dry pyjamas, was busy wringing out his wings in the kitchen sink.

But at that moment, a burnt smell and a bubbling noise reminded Nina that she'd put some soup on the stove.

'Oh no,' she cried. 'Why did I leave the lid on the pan?' The soup had spilled out of the sides and made **a horrible steamy mess** on the hob.

'I'll help you!' said Ravi, dropping his wings and leaping forward. He got a cloth and wiped up the bits of soup that had spilled on to the floor.

'Oh dear, oh dear.' Nina wrung her hands. 'Sit down, sit down at the table!' she said. 'I'll clear this up.'

Helga, who had come back into the room with neatly brushed but still damp hair and a pair of pyjamas with the face of Jeremy Pont on them, stared at the pot on the stove. She nudged Olivia, who was still marvelling at how strange it was to see Nina here.

'**Look**,' said Helga meaningfully. 'At *that*. The pot boiled over!'

'We know!' said Ravi from the floor.

'No,' said Helga slowly. '**The pot boiled over!**'

Ravi and Olivia exchanged glances and shook their heads.

'What?' said Olivia.

'I'm thinking,' said Helga, slowly sitting down at the table.

Nina took off Olivia's wet coat, wrapped her in a blanket and bustled her into a seat at the table. She took the damp, soupy cloth from Ravi. 'Join your friends,' the nanny said firmly.

But Helga still looked lost in her own world. Outside, the storm had started to scream. The windows were juddering in their panes as huge flashes of lightning lit up the garden so brightly it was as though they could see every blade of grass on the lawn, but in black and white instead of green.

'Go on, Olly!' said Ravi. 'What have you got to tell us?'

'Oh, yeah,' said Olivia. She cleared her throat. 'ORHI!' she said in a more commanding voice, startling even Helga into paying attention.

'Present and correct!' said Ravi with a smile.

'Breaking news!' announced Olivia, using a phrase she'd heard on the radio. She was secretly rather pleased – she'd been saving it for the right occasion. 'I've just found out the new group of grown-ups at the palace also can't see the real Alez! Because everything looks beautiful from up there!'

Behind her, Nina's movements slowed down, and she turned a bit red.

'What?' said Helga suspiciously, snapping out of her dream. 'Where did you hear this?'

'We got thrown out of the palace because

Jeremy Pont and . . . well, you know who I mean,' Olivia said to Helga. She didn't want to be rude about Helga's mum, especially not while she was wrapped in her blanket and eating her soup. 'They said Alez needed fixing. But they're not doing it! And no one else is either. It's just more grown-ups pretending everything is OK.'

Helga bristled. 'If you mean my mums,' she said crossly, 'they work very hard. All the time! They do loads of stuff trying to make society a better place. Like hospitals and schools and things.'

'Er, yes, that's true,' murmured Nina from behind her. 'That's definitely true.'

'But they're not doing anything about the **weather!**' said Olivia. 'And they should be! Because that affects everything else! **Look!**' She pointed out of the window at just the moment that lightning struck a tree in the garden. It fell heavily away from the house, crashing into the

garden. The roof tiles sounded as though they were dancing a jig above their heads, clanging and rattling as even the house itself seemed to brace itself against the tempest.

'Oh,' said Helga in surprise. 'You could do better than my mums? You know how to fix the weather?'

'**Yes!**' said Olivia. 'Well, no, not exactly. But I've got an idea.' She held up **a drawing** she had prepared in her notebook.

'I don't get it!' said Ravi, pointing at the picture. 'Why have you put a volcano in the middle of Alez? Is there one?'

'I'm not sure,' confessed Olivia. 'I asked my Uncle Cassander and he said there were no volcanoes in Alez. But maybe one just popped up without us knowing it? And it's pumping carbon dioxide into the atmosphere?'

Helga piped up. 'No,' she said with great certainty. 'Volcanoes take millions of years to form, so if there was one, we'd know about it. My mums let me use the internet to find out for our school homework.'

'So if it's not a volcano,' said Olivia, who knew what Helga was saying felt right, 'then *something* in that area is sending gas into the atmosphere, which my hypothesis says is making everything warmer than it should be. It's putting **a thick blanket** round the Earth again, just like it did millions of years ago! And that's somehow connected to everything going wrong. Whatever it is, maybe it's here?' She'd picked the middle of the forest for her volcano drawing, and she hoped they wouldn't ask her why as she didn't really know. It just looked right.

'With our new investigation information, we now know that grown-ups think if they ignore any problems then they aren't happening. It doesn't matter if it's a king and queen or if it's a government. They're still grown-ups and they're still doing nothing about the wrong weather!'

'On point!' said Ravi, impressed. 'You *are* a detective!'

'No,' said Olivia. 'We are **investigators**, and this is our **first real investigation**. It's our job to work out not just what's going on but what the reason is for it. I don't know the reason yet, but I'm starting to have an idea.'

She held up another drawing from her notebook.

'What is it?' asked Ravi curiously.

'It's a greenhouse!' said Olivia. 'You can grow things in it that wouldn't grow outside because the glass lets in the sunshine but traps **the warm air** inside.'

THE GREENHOUSE EFFECT

by Mira Adhikari

HAVE YOU EVER BEEN INSIDE A GREENHOUSE AND NOTICED THAT IT'S MUCH HOTTER INSIDE IT THAN OUTSIDE?

That's because the glass walls of the greenhouse trap heat from the Sun's rays and stop them escaping, keeping the greenhouse toasty warm for the plants to grow, even during the night and in winter. Earth has its own version of a greenhouse, but instead of glass walls keeping the heat in, it is gases in our atmosphere like carbon dioxide, water vapour and methane that do this.

SO, HOW EXACTLY DO GREENHOUSE GASES KEEP THE EARTH WARM?

During the day, energy from the Sun reaches the planet's surface, warming it. The Earth then releases this heat energy back into the atmosphere. Greenhouse gases are special compared to other gases in the atmosphere, like oxygen and nitrogen, because they're able to absorb this heat and stop some of it escaping out to space. When they absorb this energy, their molecules vibrate more, holding on to the heat for a while and eventually releasing it in any direction, including back down to the Earth's surface, which warms it up more. The greenhouse gases act as a blanket, allowing our planet's surface and atmosphere to hang on to more of the heat than it would otherwise be able to.

Without these gases, all of the Earth's energy would be released straight back out to space and our planet would be an icy −18°C, much too cold to support life! We need greenhouse gases to keep our planet warm enough to live on, but greenhouse gas levels are increasing from human-related activities, and starting to trap more heat than we need. This is changing the climate in different parts of the world, causing more droughts and heatwaves in some areas and worse flooding in others, as well as a whole host of other problems. The key is keeping things in balance, with just the right amount of greenhouse gases in the atmosphere to keep the Earth a safe place for everyone.

'Because,' said Helga triumphantly, who had clearly been waiting for her moment. 'Heat rises, as Doctor Mizuki showed us with her experiment. It's like the pot of soup on the stove! It boiled over because the heat couldn't get out . . .'

'Because it had a lid on it!' said Ravi delightedly. 'That's why it made a horrible mess of the kitchen!'

'Yes!' said Helga. 'The whole world is like that pot of soup! Heat is rising but there's **a lid** on it which means the heat can't go away – so it's making everything **boil over!**'

'You're so clever!' said Olivia, striking her damp palm on her forehead. 'Yes! The carbon dioxide has put a blanket over the Earth, just like the lid of the pan, and now everywhere is like my greenhouse at the palace! We're living in a giant greenhouse! Or a huge pan of hot soup.' She shook her head. 'We have to *do* something!'

'But what?' asked Ravi. 'We're just kids!'

'We need,' said Olivia decisively, 'to go and take a look at **the forest**! We have to find some evidence and **that's** where it is, I just **know** it. Doctor Mizuki said that trees breathe in carbon dioxide and breathe it out as oxygen. But we think there is too much carbon dioxide in the atmosphere so the world is getting too warm, and the heat can't escape. Maybe the trees have stopped breathing! But why would they do that? We have to go and see.'

'In the storm?' said Ravi, pointing to the window. Even though it was completely dark now outside, it was a thick blackness full of movement and scary noises as the storm kept attacking everything in its path. 'Can't we just look on the internet?' said Ravi. 'Maybe someone posted pictures?'

'No!' said Helga. 'It's illegal to post photos of the area outside the city of Alez. Even if someone did, they'd be taken down straight away.'

'Why?' said Olivia.

'Because it's a **forbidden** area. My mum told me. Ordinary people aren't allowed to go there.'

'We're not ordinary!' piped up Ravi. 'She's an ex-princess and *you're* the next president.'

'If we can't get to the forest and we can't find any information on the internet, what can we do?' said Olivia slowly. 'We really need to make observations to see if my hypothesis is correct!' She searched her memory. 'I know! There's a **lookout tower!** I remember going when I was really tiny. If we can get there we can see out over the forest. And,' she added, 'I can check on my angel tree too.'

'How are we going to get to the old lookout?' said Helga. 'Do you even know where it is?'

'Of course,' said Olivia. 'I know every tiny bit of Alez from my book of maps!'

'You still need to travel there,' said Helga. 'How are you going to do that?'

'I know someone –' said Olivia.

'Who?' Ravi interrupted. 'You don't know anyone!'

'I do know people!' protested Olivia. 'My

Uncle Cassander! I bet he knows how to get there. He's just come over from his island to stay with us, but I haven't seen him yet because I had to go to school today.'

'He'd take us?' said Ravi doubtfully. Most grown-ups he knew always said no when you asked them to do anything fun.

'**I can't go!**' said Helga quickly. 'I can't break the law! My mums always say I have to be a model citizen. Otherwise, I'll let myself down and disappoint them.'

Olivia thought about what her parents told her: to do her duty to Alez. 'It isn't wrong,' said Olivia. 'It's part of **a science experiment**. It's schoolwork.'

But she thought of Dr Mizuki and her worried face when she asked her about greenhouses and carbon dioxide. There must be something going on that Dr Mizuki couldn't talk about.

'But don't come if you don't want to,' she said

generously to Helga. 'Ravi and I can investigate and tell you later!'

'Tell us what?' Nina was hovering over their shoulders.

'Whether Ravi and Olivia can stay for a sleepover!' said Helga, pleased with her second stroke of genius. 'Please, Nina! Please, can they?'

Nina looked out of the window at the deepening storm. 'No one is leaving the house in this weather,' she said. 'Your mums are going to have to stay up at the palace too tonight,' she said to Helga. 'There's flooding on all the roads and a rockslide. Don't worry – they're quite safe! They'll call you in the morning.'

CHAPTER 8

Paragona was so relieved when Nina phoned to tell her Olivia was safe and sound and would stay overnight at the white house that she quite forgot to be cross with Nina for working for people she considered her arch-enemies.

Instead, she said that Olivia's Uncle

Cassander had arrived that morning, luckily before the storm, and would collect Olivia the next day. They couldn't reach Ravi's mum – he said her phone would be on silent when she was working the night shift, but they left a message for her, which Ravi said would be OK.

Olivia had hoped the sleepover would be a chance for more detective work by night, preparing for the exciting arrival of Uncle Cassander in the morning and possibly the kind of midnight feast she had read about in books.

But she didn't realize how tired she was until she got into bed. Despite the storm hammering at the windows, she felt **cosy and safe** here with Nina and her two friends. She knew they had an important mystery to solve, but even so she slipped away into the land of the sweetest dreams, where the angel tree of Alez was covered in flowers, her dad was smiling, the sky was still blue above their heads and the falling rain was clean and sweet once more.

The next morning, the three woke up very early to the sound of Nina humming a tune while something delicious-smelling sizzled in the kitchen. Outside, they heard the distinctive noise of **an old-fashioned motorbike** and a cheery 'Yello!' shouted from the driveway.

'Uncle Cassander's here!' cried Olivia. She ran outside to where her uncle, wearing a helmet and goggles, was sitting astride a vintage motorbike with a pillion seat on the back. It also had a sidecar.

The world was a different place from the night before. The sky was blue and clear, and the Sun shone brightly. But everywhere Olivia looked she saw branches wrenched from trees by the storm, twisted pieces of metal, tatty plastic bags, roof tiles, broken glass, smashed garden furniture and lakes of muddy water. The beautiful garden was completely destroyed. Great slabs of the lawn had been torn up and flung about like ripped fabric. Olivia even thought she saw a couple of **fish** in a **tree!**

Uncle Cassander whisked off his helmet, goggles and gloves, ruffled his hair and jumped off the bike, which he perched on a stand. He held both his arms out and knelt down so Olivia could run straight to him for a hug.

'Olly!' he said, wrapping his long arms round her. She sighed as he hugged her and felt the telltale signs of her eyes starting to water again. To distract herself, she peered into the sidecar.

'Did you bring the kitty-cats?' she asked.

'I brought them over from the island, yes!' he said. 'They travelled in the sidecar.'

'In a cat carrier?' asked Olivia.

'No!' said Uncle Cassander. 'That would

be way beneath their dignity!' He gave Olivia a mock disapproving look. 'They were peeking out the whole journey!'

'I bet their little faces looked so cute with their fur blowing in the wind,' said Olivia enviously. She wished she could have been in the sidecar with the kittens – she thought that would cheer her up more than anything! She had never been allowed a proper pet in the palace. Even though she had tried adopting a series of mice and frogs, they never stuck around long enough for her to get really fond of them. And they never answered to their names.

'Put this on,' said Cassander, producing a second helmet. 'Your mum says I'm to take a friend of yours home too. We'll take it slow. Some of the roads are blocked so we'll have to find a way around.'

'I know a good short cut!' said Olivia. Over the years, she had memorized the book of maps of Alez and knew every road and path that criss-crossed the kingdom that should have been hers. 'It goes via a very special place too. We want to go there first.'

'**You do?**' said Cassander. For a moment he looked surprised, and then he remembered – this was Olivia, and if she said she knew a short cut, he should listen. Although he already suspected the short cut might turn out to be not so short after all. 'You can **navigate** then,' he said.

'Cool!' said Olivia, smiling to herself with self-satisfaction. She had known Uncle Cassander would never let her down.

Ravi hadn't been on a motorbike before, so he was beside himself with excitement at the prospect of going home in the sidecar.

Nina looked doubtful as to whether this really was a good idea, especially when she realized that Olivia would be on the back of the motorbike. But Nina was also never going to say no to Uncle Cassander, who had always been her second favourite royal person and whom she trusted completely, so Olivia was allowed to put the motorbike helmet on and climb on the back.

Helga was frantic with mixed emotions – she was desperate to go with her friends but knew her mums would never agree, and she was also a little too scared of the motorbike to push the point as she usually would. Before the other two left, they had an urgent whispered conversation.

'I'll be **mission control**,' said Helga. For once, she sounded like she was almost pleading. 'Please, Olly,' she said humbly. '**Please**.'

'OK,' said Olivia nicely. 'But how do we contact Mission Control?'

'You can message me on Mum's iPad!' said Helga. 'She hasn't taken it to work! Put her number in Uncle Cassander's phone!'

Uncle Cassander was busy gossiping with

Nina, so he didn't question Olivia when she asked him to hand her his phone. Helga tapped her mum's number in under 'Mission Control' and Olivia gave her uncle back his phone with a sweet smile.

The three friends stood in a huddle together.

'Mission Control!' said Olivia. 'You stay here and be ready to help if we need you! Ravi, you're my second investigator! Eyes and ears! We have to notice everything we see, hear and even smell,' she said, remembering Dr Mizuki's words in class. 'This is really important!'

'**ORHI forever!**' The three of them had a group hug. Olivia and Ravi put their motorbike helmets on as, finally, Cassander stopped chatting to Nina and got ready to leave.

The old bike turned carefully in a circle in the big driveway in front of Helga's house, Olivia on the back and Ravi sitting in the side-car, whooping with joy as they motored slowly

out of sight. Helga waved and waved until she couldn't even hear the sound of the old bike put-putting along the mountain roads, swerving to avoid the fallen rocks and tree branches.

The three riders set off up the old winding road towards the **highest point** of Alez. Here was the old lookout, once the place from where the armies belonging to Olivia's family

would survey the coast and the mountains to check whether invaders were trying to enter the kingdom. Now it was the building from where an ex-princess and one of her best friends hoped to see the mighty forest over the crest of the hill to find out what – or who – was changing the weather above their heads.

CHAPTER 9

With Olivia guiding him from behind, Cassander drove up through the dirty clouds and into the cleaner air above, twisting along the narrow roads. He knew perfectly well the area they were crossing was out of bounds, but given the damage from the storm he also knew that if they were stopped they could claim to be forced to travel these roads because the main ones were closed due to mud and rockslides as well as flooding. They rode the sturdy old bike through farmyards, over out-of-use fields and up steep narrow paths, which oxen used to plod along to reach the top of the steep incline.

Some of the routes were so **narrow** and had such a **steep drop** down to one side that Olivia found she was holding her breath while indicating directions to Cassander by poking him in the side.

Ravi, in the sidecar, did the opposite – like the little kittens, he kept his face turned outwards and made silent screams of joy as the bike occasionally veered close enough to the edge for him to peer down into the great ravines below. He had never been outside the city of Alez, so to him it was the greatest adventure.

Olivia, who had travelled along roads like this on the ancient bus that took her and her family away from their old lives at the Palace, kept her gaze fixed firmly forward and thought carefully about what she needed to get from her trip to the lookout.

The changing noise of the engine signalled they were slowing down, so she looked around to check they were in the right place. Sure enough, Cassander had driven them to the old lookout tower, constructed centuries ago by his and Olivia's ancestors to keep a watchful eye over their lands and the angel tree. These days, it looked like **a ruin**, but Olivia hoped that the staircase inside would still be perfectly functional. She remembered her last trip there with her father, when he had still been happy, and the angel tree had been covered in flowers.

Over the years, she had asked her dad

many times to take her to the lookout again, but he had always refused, a sad look on his creased brow. As she thought about it, Olivia realized that her father's sadness hadn't started when they had left the palace, but a long time before. King Tolemy the Thirty-Second had looked stressed and worried even when he wore the crown – and now that he didn't have the robes and the fancy costumes, it was even more obvious than it was before. But why? Why had her dad been a sad king? She sighed. Why did feelings keep making an appearance when all she wanted to do was solve a science mystery?

Cassander clunked the heavy bike to a standstill and Ravi finally let out the **shout of happiness** he'd been trying to hold in through the whole journey.

'That was the best!' he yelled.

With Cassander's help, Olivia climbed off,

carefully removed her helmet and adjusted her glasses. She took her notebook out of her messenger bag and looked carefully at her list.

'Right, Olly,' said Cassander. 'I know you. What is this all about really?'

'It's about my hypothesis,' said Olivia.

'Knew it!' said Cassander delightedly. 'I knew you wouldn't give up! Where is the hypothesis taking us now?'

'**Up those stairs**,' said Olivia determinedly, pointing at the lookout tower. The door was closed and a sign next to the face of Jeremy Pont was plastered across it:

> *Keep out! Order of the Alez government!*
> *It is illegal to enter this building –*
> *trespassers will be prosecuted!*

Olivia paused and looked Jeremy Pont firmly in the papery eye. 'You're not doing what you

said,' she informed the poster of the president. 'You said you would make things better and you didn't! *And* you won't let anyone ask questions!'

The area around the tower was in a much worse state than Olivia remembered – old plastic bottles, cans, bags of rubbish and bits of paper littered the nearby land. The ancient stone blocks had been covered in pro-government graffiti, some of it really quite rude. It looked uncared for and unloved but, as Cassander pointed out, fortunately it also looked **completely abandoned**, as though no one now used it and it was being left to collapse gently back into the hilltop on which it was perched.

'Can we get in?' said Ravi doubtfully, trying the door handle – which came off in his hand. 'Are we allowed?'

'Yes,' said Cassander, producing a penknife out of his pocket. 'And also, no.'

'Are we going to?' asked Ravi, now very excited about doing something that might not be strictly permitted.

'Absolutely,' said Cassander firmly. He flipped open his penknife and pushed the blade into the lock to open the old wooden door. It splintered, as the wood was soft from age and lack of upkeep. 'After all,' said Cassander, 'once upon a time this door and everything you see around you belonged to Princess Olivia here, so I really think she has the right to have this door opened, if she commands me.'

'I do command you,' said Olivia solemnly. 'Even though I command you **in the name of science**, not in the name of Majesty.'

Cassander wrenched the creaking door open and made a low bow at the same time as Ravi dropped into a deep curtsey.

'Professor Olivia Alez,' said Cassander courteously. 'Please pass through this humble doorway in the name of science.'

Nodding seriously, Olivia walked through the doorway to the flight of stone stairs which, despite the decay of the outside of the building, looked exactly as she remembered them from all those years ago. They looked perfectly solid and safe, so she started to clamber up the winding staircase, her uncle and her friend behind her.

The three of them were so busy climbing upwards that none of them noticed the red eye of a little camera. It caught their movements as they ascended to the top of the old lookout, to gaze on the land of Alez to see if they could work out why it had gone so very wrong.

CHAPTER 10

Once at the top of the tower, it was still early enough that the mists had not yet cleared so they could see very little beyond the immediate land around the tower, which was also plastic-strewn and scrubby, the patchy grass fighting to keep its roots in the crumbling earth.

'We can't **see** anything!' objected Ravi.

'But we can **smell** something,' said Olivia, wrinkling her nose in disgust. A dank stinky waft of air which smelled of old socks, rotten eggs and burnt plastic blew up towards the three of them, causing them all to flap their hands in front of their faces.

'Look,' said Cassander, pointing to the east. The Sun, rising in the sky above the hills, was sending long slants of light down, piercing the mist. Bit by bit, the landscape emerged from the haze as the sunlight chased away the wisps of cloud. But where Olivia expected to see the deep-green forests and rushing streams she had loved so much, like she had seen in old books about Alez and when she had been up here with her father, she saw something **very different** indeed. She was so taken aback her mouth fell open and she thought her eyes might fall out of her face!

Ravi gasped loudly as the mists rolled back and even Cassander had to hold on to the edge of the parapet to steady himself from the shock. What they saw, as the blanket of mist revealed what lay underneath, was **a wasteland**. The only trees that remained were blackened, **charred stumps**. Small fires had broken out here and there, some on the ground, some in black metal dustbins. To one side loomed heaps of old plastic, bags, broken household items and old clothes – the huge piles were almost large enough to look like the formation of a new range of mountains.

On the other side, where there once had been an ancient peaceful woodland, stood **vast factories**, belching out great burps of black smoke. The wind picked up the dirty air and blew it towards the city behind them. A lake that Olivia had last seen as an oval of brilliant blue, sending clear rushing streams towards the city,

was now a murky, dark pond, half covered in violently green algae blooms strangling the life of the ecosystem below. None of this had been visible from the palace where Olivia had lived, which was nestled in a crook of the mountains, facing the ocean.

Worst of all, where Alez's special angel tree

had once flowered, there was just an old tree
with bare branches.

Olivia was horrified. '**Our tree!**' she said,
her voice breaking with a sob.

Ravi peered at the tree more closely and saw
one small pink flower blooming on a fragile
outstretched branch. He nudged his friend.

'Olly,' he said. 'There's one flower on that tree, just a tiny one.'

Olivia shook her head. 'I can't see it,' she said sadly.

Cassander pointed out over the damaged land, which stretched as far as the mountains on the far side of Alez, right up to the glacier.

'That glacier used to come right down to the foot of the mountain,' he said in a shocked voice.

'It looks like an **ice cube** now!' said Ravi in horror. 'Perched on top of the mountain. Not a glacier at all.'

'It's so tiny!' said Olivia. 'Why is it so small?'

'It's **melted**,' said Cassander grimly. 'And look – those mountains used to have snow on them! And now they're just bare rock.'

They all looked at the jagged mountain peaks, bare and craggy without their soft blanket of white snow.

'I think that mountain,' said Ravi, pointing, 'fell down in the storm.'

'It looks like it's crying,' said Olivia. Along the mountain range, they noticed a strange pattern of teardrop-shaped rocks on it, leading down into the valley.

CLIMATE CHANGE AND EXTREME WEATHER

by Dr Tom Matthews

HEAT RISES

As humans increase the amount of greenhouse gases (like carbon dioxide) in our atmosphere, more energy is trapped on Earth. And we have already trapped a lot of energy - enough to power over 100 billion kitchen ovens non-stop for over fifty years! A result of this build-up is that the temperature worldwide has increased by about 1°C in the past 170 years. Such global warming makes uncomfortably hot weather more common. It also makes it more likely that we will experience record-breaking temperatures.

These changes are a problem almost everywhere that humans inhabit because hot weather can make us sick, stop us from sleeping, and limit our ability to work, study or exercise. Countries with already hot climates face the greatest threat because just a little bit of heating can make it dangerously warm a lot more often.

RAIN GETS HEAVIER

A warmer atmosphere can also hold more water. To get a sense for this, imagine what it feels like when it's just the right temperature indoors (about 20°C). The air in an average-sized living room at this temperature would be able to hold over 700ml of water vapour – enough to fill around two Coke cans once turned into liquid water (condensed). Now hold your hand in front of your mouth and feel the air that you breathe out (slowly). Unless you're somewhere very hot, you will notice that it's quite a bit warmer than the air around you. If the same living room was heated to this temperature (about 35°C), the air could hold around 1,800ml of water – enough to fill almost six Coke cans!

When there is very heavy rain, the atmosphere drops nearly all its water. This means that the more water there is in the atmosphere to begin with, the heavier the rain can be. Thinking back to the role of air temperature, it should be clear why heavy rain events become more common and more extreme as the climate warms. We can imagine making the floor much wetter with our six cans of water condensed from the hotter living room than we can with the two cans collected from our cooler one!

FIRE WEATHER BECOMES MORE COMMON

The extra water that the air holds as it warms must come from somewhere, so parts of the Earth's surface that are already dry get even drier as the hotter air draws more water away. Hot air and dry ground make ideal conditions for fires, especially if combined with strong winds. This type of weather caused some very big wildfires in California recently, including one that threatened the world's biggest tree (named General Sherman) in 2021 – a giant that is thousands of years old and nearly the same height as the Statue of Liberty!

Fortunately, General Sherman survived, this time, but the mighty tree – along with many others in vulnerable regions worldwide – faces a growing threat from more frequent forest fires under climate warming.

THE STRONGEST STORMS BECOME EVEN STRONGER

Tropical cyclones (also called hurricanes and typhoons) are the most powerful storms (or 'weather systems') on our planet. They release an amount of energy equivalent to thousands of nuclear bombs exploding, as they bring very heavy rain, extremely strong winds and deadly storm surges (when the ocean floods the land). They can also be very dangerous. The worst we know about sadly killed over 500,000 people when it struck the country now known as Bangladesh in 1970.

Climate change causes tropical cyclones to change in several important ways. First (and maybe surprisingly), it favours slightly fewer storms overall. But the second change is not such good news, because warming causes more of the storms that do form to grow into the strongest category (with the fastest winds), and record-breaking strength becomes more likely. Climate change also causes tropical cyclones to produce heavier rain as the air becomes hotter (and can therefore hold more water - as we just learned). Their storm surges can go further inland too - not just because faster winds blow the water harder against the coast, but because sea-level rise is another impact of climate change, so the water is already creeping further on to the shore.

'A rockfall,' said her uncle. 'It probably collapsed in the storm with no ice to hold it in place. And look! There's practically a town there!'

He pointed to an area where a series of flat-roofed buildings had been constructed. Dotted around the buildings were pieces of heavy machinery.

'It's **horrible!**' said Olivia. 'The forest has gone! And the angel tree! And there's nothing but dirty smoke coming out of those factory chimneys. Is that –' she paused, as everything fell into place – 'where all the carbon dioxide is coming from?'

'Yes,' said a voice behind them. 'It isn't as pretty as a forest full of royal princes, princesses and unicorns, is it now?'

The three of them whipped round. None of them had heard the footsteps coming up the stairs, nor realized they had company, until it was too late. Standing behind them, heavy and smirking, stood the unmistakable figure of Jeremy Pont. Lined up behind him were a group of police.

'**Guards**,' said Jeremy menacingly. '**Arrest these three**.'

'On what charges?' said Cassander bravely. Behind him, he felt rather than saw a small hand take his mobile phone.

'**Treason!**' replied Jeremy. 'You have been talking about the Republic of Alez in a way that is expressly forbidden in one of the laws I passed recently – if only you had been keeping up. And there's a charge of breaking and entering government property within the Forbidden Zone. I think you'll find both charges carry a pretty long sentence. Frisk him,' Jeremy said to the guard. 'And take any communication devices you find on him.'

Olivia froze. She stood stock-still, but her brain was whirring as she tried to think what to do now.

Cassander stepped forward in front of the two kids to protect them, but he was swiftly grabbed by one of the larger guards who wrestled him to the side, leaving Jeremy face to face with Olivia, with Ravi hovering behind her.

Jeremy cast a look at Ravi, over Olivia's head and noted the fairy wings, still pinned on his back. Jeremy decided to ignore Ravi, who was tapping on Cassander's phone, concentrating instead on the small figure of the girl whose house he had taken and made into his very own home on that sunny day not so very long ago.

'**Well, well, well**,' said Jeremy. '**We meet again**, Princess Olivia.'

'I'm not Princess Olivia!' said Olivia. 'As you well know!'

'Then who are you?' said Jeremy in an amused tone of voice, his mocking smile playing across his face.

'I,' began Olivia, drawing herself up to

her full height – which was still not very tall – and pushing her glasses back up her nose. She decided to use her best scary voice in the manner of her great-grandmother, the grande marquessa. And finally the voice came out, just as she wanted it to sound! 'I am a scientist and a guardian of Alez! And I demand to know – **what have you done to our country?!**'

CHAPTER 11

What have I done to this country?' exclaimed Jeremy, letting out a dry laugh. 'What have *I* done? Oh, Olivia, you may not be a princess, but you are priceless!'

'This land,' said Olivia fiercely, 'used to be green and beautiful, with clean water coming from the glacier, air that kids could breathe safely, and lots of animals and insects. And now it's just factories and garbage!'

'Yes, it's true,' said Jeremy, recovering himself. 'The fabled land of your ancestors is no more, my precious little queen that never will be. And do you know why that is?'

Olivia felt unsure for a second as she met his cold blue eyes.

'Let me tell you, O jewel of the Alez dynasty,' said Jeremy. 'Countries, my dear girl, need *money*. They need to pay for things, like roads, schools, governments, houses for children to live in. Food for people to eat. Lighting for streets. It's **terribly expensive**, you know. And once upon a time, it had to pay for a royal family too!'

'What's that got to do with the forest?' said Olivia.

'Forests don't make any money,' said Jeremy. 'Trees – they just sit there, growing. They don't make a contribution to the national economy. But factories do: processing waste from other countries, producing products, creating energy, mining for gold or rare elements. These important things make money, lots of money for the Alez people. Once upon a time, every penny went to your family, you know.'

'My father didn't do this!' said Olivia angrily.

'Not quite in the way you see it now,' said Jeremy smoothly. 'But he fell asleep on his throne and he didn't keep an eye on what was happening to his country! He let people take decisions on his behalf without checking to see what they were really doing.' He gave a very **nasty smile**.

'You were one of those people!' shouted Cassander. 'You told Tolemy you would fix everything, bring income into the country to help the poor! You claimed you were building a new future for Alez with projects that would be clean and safe. It's pretty clear you were lying! **Olly**, don't be **fooled!**'

'Your father let things slip,' said Jeremy to Olivia with a smirk. Olivia felt absolutely floored. She had suspected her parents had no real idea what was going on in Alez, but then she wondered – had her father known? Was that why he had been so sad?

'Your father never took any notice of what we actually did. We built this industrial area during his reign, and then when the money started pouring in it seemed such a waste for it to go to him, so we decided it was time to have a change of ruler and let the country as a whole profit. For the good of the people,' he added solemnly.

'And so you thought,' said Olivia, who was so angry now that she was using a scary voice that was entirely her own, 'it was OK to make it so that kids can't go out to play because **the air** is

too dirty to breathe, we can't drink the water because it would make us sick, there's **nowhere green** for us to play on, people don't have enough food, and everyone is **sad** and **miserable** because you've messed up the world we live in? You thought it was worth doing those things just so you could have more money! And now you live in our palace, and because you can't see all this from there, you don't even care.'

'Of course not,' said Jeremy angrily. 'That's not what we wanted for the new Alez! We are making **a better, fairer world** and to say anything else is an act of disobedience against the new government, which is punishable by lifetime imprisonment.'

'That's why,' said Olivia, who wasn't remotely frightened now, 'you don't let anyone talk about carbon dioxide and what it does to our world! You won't let kids ask questions about it at school or look at stuff on the internet where we might learn about it. Because *you* release carbon dioxide and other things –' she pointed to the factory chimneys – 'into the atmosphere and it makes these bad changes happen. Doctor Mizuki says that trees breathe carbon dioxide and turn it into oxygen, but you've cut them down so that can't happen.' She felt very clear now. 'We're not allowed to know about greenhouses gases either because –' she thought about the greenhouse at the palace – 'greenhouses keep the heat in, and I think that the gases you are putting into our atmosphere are trapping the heat inside it. **That's why** Alez is **getting hotter**. The water is drying up because it's too warm for the glacier, and now it's almost completely melted away!'

'And,' burst out Ravi, 'that means there's **no clean water!** We had that huge storm last night! We never know if it's going to be too hot or too cold!'

'Because of the rising temperature, the weather can't work like it's supposed to!' said Olivia triumphantly. She'd just worked out **the missing** piece of **the puzzle.** 'You've made the weather go wrong!'

Jeremy Pont's face had turned puce by now. He looked like he might explode, like the volcano Olivia had learned about in school.

'This is **an outrage!**' he spluttered. 'Guards, seize these children and take them away, with this traitor over here.' He pointed at Cassander, who had been gagged by now and was unable to speak or move his hands.

But just at that moment, they heard running feet coming up the staircase at great speed, then a figure charged through the door to the parapet and threw herself between Ravi and Olivia and Jeremy Pont.

It was Helga's mum, Gretchen Sparks, with the familiar figure of Helga emerging cautiously behind her on to the parapet to give them both a thumbs up. Olivia thought she might cry again, but told her eyes very strictly this was not the moment! For once, she didn't need to think about the grande marquessa – she was now able to be fierce all on her own.

'Gretchen!' said Jeremy in amazement. 'What are you doing here?'

'Jeremy!' said Helga's mum. 'You've gone far enough! It's **time to stop!**'

'Stop what?' said Jeremy. He did not look best pleased.

'You seem,' said Gretchen, recovering her composure, 'to be trying to arrest two children because they have pointed out to you something you should have known, and you should have done something about.'

'These children,' said Jeremy, 'are traitors!'

'**Rubbish**,' snorted Gretchen. 'They are friends of my daughter from school! Don't be ridiculous.'

'One of them is Princess Olivia!' said Jeremy.

Olivia never thought she'd be happy to see Gretchen Sparks again, but suddenly found that there was no one else she would rather have come up the steps from the tower at that exact moment.

'I don't care!' shouted Gretchen incredibly loudly. Even the guards flinched. Ravi thought he could hear her voice echoing around the valley below. 'It doesn't matter! What matters is that everyone **works together** to try and solve these problems and make Alez a healthy and safe place for these kids to grow up in! I've followed you loyally for so many years because I believed you wanted to make this a better country for everybody, but now you're ruining the environment in order to make profits for yourself and your friends! You kept me and my wife so busy solving the day-to-day problems that you couldn't be bothered to deal with, that we didn't pay attention to the most important problem that exists – the **change in the climate!** I'm super embarrassed that I hadn't noticed. I don't think I'll ever recover! But thank goodness **my clever daughter** and **her brilliant friends** figured it out for themselves! And now this has to stop!'

Gretchen, at that moment, looked absolutely terrifying. Her eyes flashed. Even Jeremy looked quelled. His trusted assistant turning on him was the last thing he had ever expected to see, especially not when he found himself up a tower with an ex-princess and her formerly princely uncle, plus a boy with fairy wings on his back.

'Come on, Jeremy,' she chided, sounding as though she was speaking to Helga. 'Once upon a time, there was birdsong in Alez. We could go to the beach and swim in the sea. We could drink the water, before the glacier melted. The sun shone and the rain came, but at the times when we expected it. People could grow their own food. We didn't live with mountains of garbage, poisoning our environment with factory smoke. We lived in a wonderful place. Isn't it time at least we tried to do so again? Don't we owe these kids a **future?**'

Jeremy looked shaken to the core. He humbly lowered his eyes.

'What do you want me to do?' he muttered.

'Ask the kids,' said Gretchen. 'After all, from

what my daughter tells me, it sounds like they know more than we do!'

Jeremy turned towards the two children and motioned to the guards to let them go and then, reluctantly, gave the nod to let Cassander be freed. Rubbing his wrists, Cassander came forward to stand behind the two kids, now joined by Helga.

'How did you get here?' Olivia whispered to Helga.

'Ravi messaged me!' said Helga. 'He said you were in trouble at the lookout tower and we needed to come straight away! Nina got in touch with Mum and we got here as fast as we could.'

'**Great work!**' said Olivia, nudging Ravi.

He smiled back at her. 'Anything for you, princess.'

'So, kids,' said Jeremy in a tired voice. He gazed out across the land of Alez, and even he had to admit to himself that it really didn't look very nice. 'What is it that you want?'

'We want . . .' Ravi piped up. For a horrible moment, Olivia thought he was going to ask for something truly random. But he didn't let her down. '. . . to make the future a place we want to live in!'

'And how are you going to do that?' Jeremy asked them in a weary voice.

'You can **begin**,' said Olivia, 'by **replanting** the **trees**. And that way we can start to make the weather go right.'

THE IMPORTANCE OF TREES

by Dr Isabel Fendley

Trees are a very important part of the environment as they provide a habitat (place to live) for many birds, bugs and other animals. Trees also provide food for animals that eat their leaves, fruits or bark.

Trees strongly affect the air in the atmosphere. Instead of eating food, trees and other plants use a process called photosynthesis to make energy. Photosynthesis combines carbon dioxide from the air, water and energy from sunlight together to make energy for the tree.

The carbon dioxide from the air is split into carbon and oxygen, and the oxygen is released back into the air. The oxygen breathed in by animals (including humans) comes from plants.

The carbon produced by photosynthesis is stored in the tree's stems, leaves and roots. After the tree dies, some of this carbon is released back into the atmosphere through decomposition, and some of the carbon stays in the ground as a part of the soil.

Trees live a long time and can grow very large, storing a lot of carbon over their lifetimes. As a result, the carbon stored in trees can stay out of the atmosphere for a long time – often more than a hundred years. As a result, planting more trees is one way to remove carbon dioxide from the atmosphere and decrease the amount of global warming.

EPILOGUE

Olivia sat in the tiny apartment, still known as the Royal Residence, and thought about everything that had happened since she left the real royal palace. She unlocked her notebook and sat Citizen George the bear next to her as she chewed the end of her pencil.

ADDITIONAL CONCLUSIONS

INVESTIGATION ONE – The Wrong Weather

1. Thanks to our hypothesis, we worked out that the world was getting hotter because of warming gases like carbon dioxide being sent into the atmosphere. This put a blanket round our world and meant that when the heat rose it got stuck, and so everywhere just got hotter and hotter. And made the weather go wrong! We now know that because of the heat trapped inside the Earth's atmosphere, there was more energy in the weather system and this caused the big storms and the other wrong weather we've been living with.

2. We also found out that the trees, which would have used up some of the carbon dioxide to breathe, had been cut down, making the problem worse. The big angel tree of Alez looked completely dead when I first saw it, but it had one tiny flower on it, which Ravi says means we still have hope!

3. We discovered that grown-ups were ignoring the problem of the wrong weather and pretending it wasn't really that bad. They were too busy doing stuff that isn't as important as the future. Since our investigation, the grown-ups have promised to listen to us more because we know what's going on and they don't. They've made a good start, I suppose, but we still have to keep an eye on them. Helga's mum is now the president because Jeremy Pont left after

making such a mess of giving Alez a better future. Gretchen Sparks asked Dr Mizuki from school to work with her when she's not too busy teaching, and said it's OK for us to learn about climate change now.

4. Weirdly, it turns out that grown-ups spend a lot of time thinking about their feelings when they should be thinking about science. BUT – surprise! – it turns out that feelings are important too (although not as important as science, I still think). Mr V arranged for me to talk to the school counsellor, who said my dad feels very sad and that makes it hard for him to have a proper life. We're going to help Dad talk about how he feels, so he can get back to being normal Dad and stop sleeping and crying all day. Helga's mums came round to talk to Mum and Dad about the 'palace

revolution' and to say they were sorry we lost
our home and everything else but that they
must be very proud of me and my friends
for helping the future of Alez! Mum and Dad
were quite smiley about it all and Dad didn't
cry, so I was proud of them too. Mum said she
wanted all her titles back if no one was using
them these days, but Gretchen Sparks pulled
a funny face, so I don't think that's going to
happen . . .

5. My mum has discovered the internet! She's
setting up a shop to sell tiaras online! This is
cool because it keeps her busy and now I can
use the internet too.

6. Uncle Cassander has gone back to the
island with the kitty-cats ☹. He says we can
come and stay next school holiday! YAY!

7. Ravi is super happy. His dad came home and is going to set up a community vegetable garden at school with my dad when he feels better! I've given Ravi my main princess crown so he can wear it whenever he wants.

8. Helga is still president of ORHI because she needs to get in some important practice at being a president. But she's also realized she needs to allow more people to join our science society because we can't do everything on our own. We're going to move on to our next investigation very soon – we just need to find our next mystery to solve . . .

GLOSSARY

There may be some terms used within this book that are new to you, or where you want to check the meaning. And if you talk about the story with your friends, or read more about the issues it raises, you might find some other new words or terms – scientific language isn't always easy to understand! Here are just a few definitions to help . . . with a little bit more information too.

ATMOSPHERE (OF THE EARTH)

A term to describe the air that surrounds our planet, the air that we breathe. There are a number of different gases in our atmosphere.

CARBON

A hugely important chemical element, one of the building blocks of life on Earth – all known life contains some carbon.

CARBON DIOXIDE

A gas that is produced when any substance containing carbon – like coal or any other fossil fuel – is burned. It is breathed out by people and animals, and breathed in by trees.

CARBON FOOTPRINT

This is a measure of the amount of carbon released by a single person or an organization over a particular period of time, e.g., a year. For instance, if you take lots of holidays abroad, and go everywhere by car, your carbon footprint will be higher than someone who stays in this country for their holidays and walks to school. A company that makes their goods using lots of fossil fuels has a greater footprint than one using renewable energy.

CLIMATE

The weather can change from day to day, and

throughout the year it varies according to the seasons. But climate is the term used to describe the average weather over a very long time, both for a particular place (like where you live) and for the planet as a whole.

CLIMATE CHANGE

This is when the average conditions start to change. Today, the science shows that we are in a period of rapid climate change. This is mostly because of heat being trapped in Earth's atmosphere.

CLIMATE CRISIS

When we reach a point where it will be difficult to stop the changes to our climate! Melting ice caps and dying coral cannot be replaced overnight. Climate change is happening now, and if we do not take action soon to slow it down, the changes will get worse and worse.

DEFORESTATION

Trees are good for our planet, producing the oxygen we need to breathe. When trees are burned or chopped down – this is called deforestation – the carbon they store is released into our atmosphere. Forests worldwide are under threat as land is cleared for agriculture, or by logging or mining.

ECOSYSTEM

An ecosystem is a complex system of all plants, animals and other life forms and the environment in which they live – whether in the desert, mountains, forests, ice or water. The result is a natural balance, with everything working together to support life. The Earth has a number of different ecosystems, which together form a balanced planet. If one goes wrong, it can have a knock-on effect on the other systems.

EMISSIONS

Emissions is the term used to describe the release of gases such as carbon dioxide into the atmosphere. Scientists look at the small-scale – like fumes from car exhausts, or a cow farting. They also observe the larger scale by, for instance, measuring emissions from a country's factories and other industries.

EXTREME WEATHER EVENTS

When you get up each day, you have a fair idea of what sort of weather you might be facing. But the weather can go wrong. Extreme weather means big dramatic events like heatwaves, storms and flooding. As a result of global warming, there are lots more of these events all around the world, and they threaten the lives of people and animals.

FOSSIL FUELS

A general term for fuels like oil, natural gas and coal – fuels that are buried beneath the surface of the Earth. They are called fossil fuels as they are formed over hundreds of millions of years. When they are burned, they release carbon dioxide into the atmosphere, and so are a big factor in climate change.

GLACIER

A glacier is formed from fallen snow that stays in one place long enough to build up into a large, thick ice mass. Due to its size and weight, the ice begins to flow downwards – like a very slow river.

GLOBAL WARMING

This is the term used to describe the rise in the Earth's temperature. The world is now about 1.2 degrees Celsius warmer than it was before fossil fuels were used to provide heat and power for our factories, homes and cars.

GREENHOUSE GASES

Greenhouse gases – like carbon dioxide, methane and nitrous oxide – are gases that trap heat. The Sun's rays hit the surface of the Earth and the radiation bounces back into the air as heat. We need these gases to keep our planet warm – without them it would be very cold and life as we know it would die out. But too many greenhouse gases in the atmosphere can cause the planet to get too warm. Right now, our planet is warming up.

HABITAT

Where you live, and what is around you, is your local environment, or habitat. There are six main kinds of environments in the world – polar, desert, forest, fresh water, rainforests and grasslands, and oceans – and the animals, plants and people who live in these areas learn to adapt to their local habitat to survive.

HYPOTHESIS

A hypothesis is an idea of why a scientist thinks something happens. It is usually based on effects observed, e.g., the wrong sort of weather.

ICE SHEETS

An ice sheet is a type of glacier – a huge area of land ice that has taken tens of thousands of years to grow. They contain enormous amounts of frozen water. But they are now shrinking – melting – due to Earth's warmer atmosphere. This is beginning to make sea levels rise.

METHANE

Another greenhouse gas, formed when plants and animals break down and decay, e.g. in an area of marshes and bogs. Livestock also produce a lot of methane as animals like cattle, sheep and goats belch and burp! Methane is also released by termites and volcanoes, as well as by the burning of fossil fuels.

NET ZERO

Greenhouse gases caused by emissions can be balanced out by doing things like planting more trees to absorb the emissions. Ideally the two sides become equal – net zero emissions. This is a target that countries all around the world are trying to meet, hoping to slow down the rise in the world's temperature.

OXYGEN

The gas we breathe. Without oxygen, we would die. The Earth's atmosphere contains about 21% oxygen and it is continually produced by plants.

PERMAFROST

Permafrost is a name for ground that remains frozen for at least two years – some areas on Earth have been frozen for tens of thousands of years! If it melts, methane is released into the atmosphere.

PLATES (OF THE EARTH)

The rocky outer layer of the Earth – the crust – is made of pieces called plates. They are constantly moving very slowly. Where they meet, there is more risk of volcanoes and earthquakes.

RENEWABLE ENERGY

Unlike energy from fossil fuels – once used, it can't be replaced – renewable energy comes from sources that are renewed again and again. They include solar power (energy from the Sun), wind power, tidal power and geothermal power (using the heat from the Earth).

SCIENCE

Science is how we try to develop our understanding of the world and the universe we live in. All science is based on observations and experiments – tests to see if the scientists' ideas are right or not.

SEA LEVELS

Our oceans absorb heat, and as they get warmer they get bigger. This means that sea levels can rise as the water gets warmer. If the ice sheets and glaciers also melt and add a lot of water to our seas, the levels can rise even more. This could cause severe floods in some areas of the world.

SULPHUR DIOXIDE

A gas that is produced by burning fuels like coal and oil, that contain sulphur. It is a pollutant, part of smog and harmful to our health. It also comes out of volcanoes.

WEATHER; WEATHER SYSTEM

The weather is the state of our atmosphere at a particular place and time. Our personal weather is affected by things like where our country lies – places close to the equator are usually warmer, and places near the poles are colder, for instance.

ACKNOWLEDGEMENTS

I've loved starting a new series with a whole new range of characters in a totally different setting – although I missed writing about space journeys more than I expected! But it felt like time to turn my attention to everyone's favourite planet, Earth, and write about what's happening here. I'm incredibly grateful to Ruth Knowles and Emma Jones at Penguin Random House Children's for encouraging me to explore our home planet and for their invaluable and brilliant insight and support for the adventures of clever, intrepid Princess Olivia and her friends. Eternal thanks to my old friend Sue Cook for once again bringing her sharp focus to the text and to the scientific content. I'm also very grateful to Cath at Salt & Sage for their helpful insights into the text.

I am very fortunate to have the help of my wonderful agent, Rebecca Carter, and everyone at Janklow and Nesbit, UK. We've been working together for so long now, they feel like my second family. I did intend, for once, to write a book without calling on my friends in science, but that didn't happen, and this book is so much better for their contributions.

I am truly indebted and grateful to three brilliant scientists who have contributed the clear, informative and beautifully written inserts on important climate-change related phenomena for this book. They are:

Dr Isabel Fendley, Department of Earth Sciences, University of Oxford, UK
On the Rise: Sea Levels
The Importance of Trees
Volcanoes

Mira Adhikari, King's College London, UK
The Greenhouse Effect
Smog

Dr Tom Matthews, King's College London, UK
Climate Change and Extreme Weather

It means so much to me that you were prepared to take up the challenge of writing about your work for young readers, and to give them accurate, up-to-date, fascinating and accessible essays on the kind of phenomena they (and we!) hear about all the time.

Finally, I'd like to thank both my super smart niece, Olivia, who showed me what a properly scary voice should sound like, and my adorable dog of the same name for the inspiration provided. This book is not about either of you, but thank you for letting me borrow your names. I hope you're pleased with how the story has turned out.

Much love, Lucy x

DISCOVER MORE FROM LUCY AND STEPHEN HAWKING

Compiled by the creators of *GEORGE'S SECRET KEY TO THE UNIVERSE*

STEPHEN & LUCY
HAWKING

UNLOCKING
THE
UNIVERSE

EVERYTHING
YOU NEED TO
TRAVEL THROUGH
SPACE AND TIME

READY FOR YOUR NEXT ADVENTURE?

Explore the bestselling George series by Lucy & Stephen Hawking

Take a rollercoaster ride through the vastness of space and discover the mysteries of physics, science and the universe with George, Annie and a super-intelligent computer called Cosmos!

LUCY & STEPHEN
HAWKING

GEORGE AND THE BIG BANG

'LIKE A DOCTOR WHO ADVENTURE INSPIRING CURIOSITY AND AMAZEMENT' *SUNDAY TIMES*

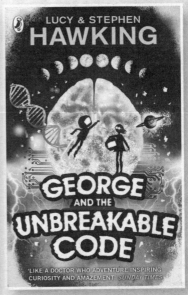

LUCY & STEPHEN
HAWKING

GEORGE AND THE UNBREAKABLE CODE

'LIKE A DOCTOR WHO ADVENTURE INSPIRING CURIOSITY AND AMAZEMENT' *SUNDAY TIMES*

LUCY & STEPHEN
HAWKING

GEORGE AND THE BLUE MOON

'LIKE A DOCTOR WHO ADVENTURE INSPIRING CURIOSITY AND AMAZEMENT' *SUNDAY TIMES*

LUCY
HAWKING

GEORGE AND THE SHIP OF TIME

'LIKE A DOCTOR WHO ADVENTURE INSPIRING CURIOSITY AND AMAZEMENT' *SUNDAY TIMES*